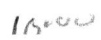

Out of Our Hearts and Minds

Also by the
Transylvania Writers' Alliance

MOUNTAIN MOODS AND MOMENTS

Copyright © 2006 Transylvania Writers' Alliance
All rights revert to authors upon publication.

Cover design by Ann Nicholson Tait

ISBN: 1-4196-3320-1

To order additional copies, please contact us.
BookSurge, LLC
www.booksurge.com
1-866-308-6235
orders@booksurge.com

Out of Our Hearts and Minds

Poetry, Prose, and Art
From
Transylvania Writers' Alliance

Sara Pacher, Editor
Catherine (Kit) Townsend Borden,
Co-editor

Illustrated by Ann Nicholson Tait

BOOKSURGE PUBLISHING
5341 Dorchester Rd.
North Charleston, SC 29418
www.booksurgepublishing.com
2006

Out of Our Hearts and Minds

TABLE OF CONTENTS

JANET BENWAY — *1*
The Scarlet Opera Cloak — 3
Grampy — 5
Chaos In The Kingdom — 6
Lament From The Lake — 7
The Grave Of The Unknown Grandmother — 8
Llama Eyes — 9
Cutting To The Chase — 10

CATHERINE (KIT) TOWNSEND BORDEN — **13**
Help! Help! There's An Elephant In My Soup! — 15
Roadside Rush — 18
Wild Things — 19
Light In The Dark — 20
Batty — 20
Orange And Purple Sunset — 21
Spring In Veracruz — 21
Libre — 21
Haiku — 22
Solace — 22
And She Laughed — 23
Woodland Walks — 23
The Wiggle-Under-The-Bed Day — 23
Beginnings — 26
Ebb Tide — 27

ALEXANDRA BURROUGHS — **29**
Notes From My Woodland Garden — 31
Seasons Change — 31
The Birdman — 32
My Haven, My Nest — 32
Middle-age Soy Latte — 33
I Love You, I Love You — 34
The Window Seat — 35

To Jean, A Poet's Poet	36
You Trimmed The Sails	36
My James Dean	37
Your Fuzzy Sweater	38
Don't Crush The Butterfly	38

WALLACE GALLOWAY — 41
At Carnton's Cemetery	43
Canto IX	45
Canto XI	46
Canto XV	50

JEAN HARRIS — 55
Stadium Concert	57
Retrogression	59
Emily	60
A Friendly Game Of Bridge	61

BEATRICE HEWSENIAN — 63
Sand	65
Meeting Boys	65

NILSA VARGAS LOBDELL — 71
Mollie Lyday McCall	73
The Saga Of The Reluctant Car	75
The Chair	76
Leaving Mother	77

MARILYN OPALOYD ONG — 81
Arizona Murphy	83
A Gift Of Knowledge	87
A True Story	90
Arrabelle Ohara	93

SARA PACHER	**95**
Gently Down The Stream	97
I'll Write Of Simple Things	97
Decades	98
Xanadu	100
Angkor Wat	101
A Mirror Poem	102
Some "Sometimes I Think" Poems	102
To An Artist In Front Of St. Patrick's	103
Have You?	104
Attitude	104
The Hair	105
BETTY J. REED	**107**
A Dazzling Autumn At The Pink Beds	109
Sister's Dilemma	113
Sister	117
ISABELLE REINER	**119**
As Night Follows Day—	121
So Do The Seasons Follow	121
Each Other	121
DEVON SMITH	**123**
The Iron Clouds	125
ANN NICHOLSON TAIT	**143**
A Fish Tale	145
Yellow	147
Breaker Monster	148
Daybreak Canvas	151
Nostalgia On Times Square	152
Saxophone	153
New Blue Tricycle	154
Night Writer's Insomnia	155
The Landscape Of His Lines	155

ELIZABETH OWEN TAYLOR	**157**
The Former Stoic	159
The End Of Innocence	159
Erin's Sonnet	160
First Kisses	160
Serendipity	161
Valentine's Day	162
Night Train To St. Petersburg	162
The Beginning Of Wisdom	163
Dream Quests	163
Seize The Ripeness	165
A Distinction	165
One September Morning	165
(9. 11. 2001)	165
Daily Spectacles	166
The Orgy	167
Seasonal Sensories	168
Homage To Bare Trees	169
ANTHONY TINSLEY	*171*
Churning	173
Papa	173
ANNE HARDING WOODWORTH	**175**
The Audit	177

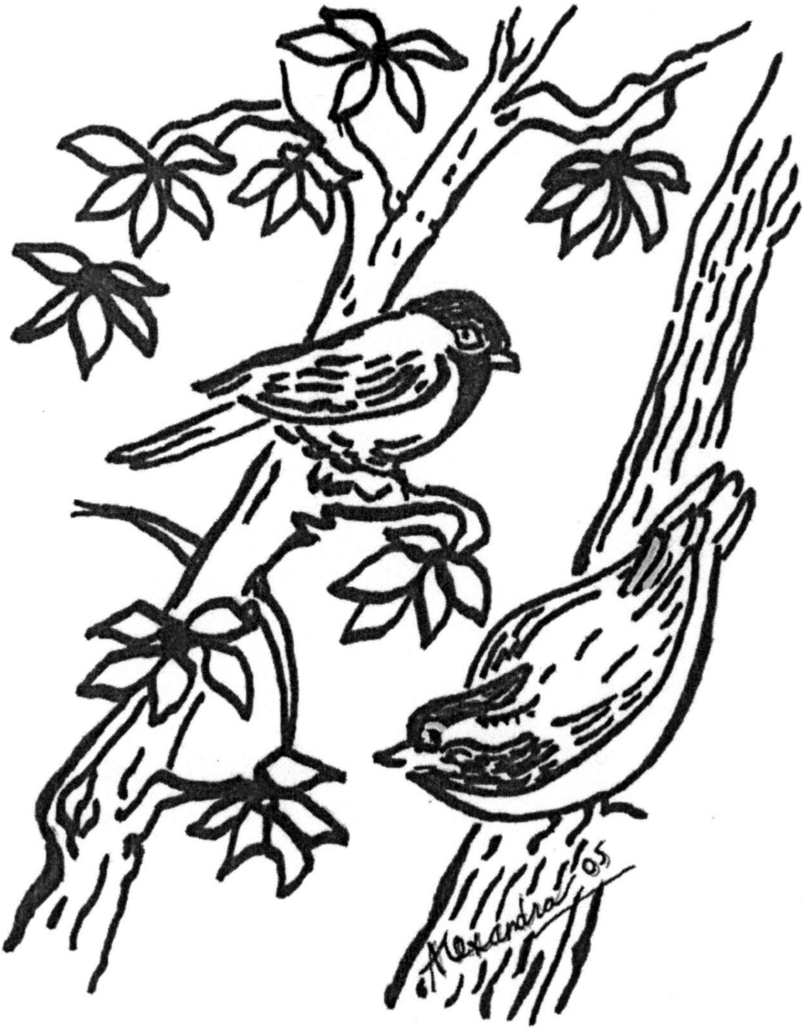
Alexandra '05

ACKNOWLEDGMENTS

First, we thank BookSurge Publishing for offering a "prize" that funded the expenses of this book up to print-ready status. At a publisher's gathering at Creative 101 art gallery in Brevard, North Carolina, Ray Henley's name was drawn to receive this prize. Ray, not being a writer himself, very graciously offered the prize to friend and TWA member Janet Benway. Janet, in turn, offered the prize to the Transylvania Writers' Alliance. We owe thanks to both Janet and Ray for their generosity. Then, when our editor, Sara Pacher, was called away unexpectedly to the West Coast, Catherine (Kit) Townsend Borden jumped in to keep the book on schedule and more than earned the title of co-editor. We thank Ann Nicholson Tait for her fine illustrations and our dynamic cover. We also want to thank Howard Friedman and Alexandra Burroughs for their invaluable technical work on the computer.

INTRODUCTION

More than a decade ago, a small group of writers in Transylvania County, North Carolina, advertised their intention to found a writing group to tap the abundant talent amongst the citizens of this charming region in the Blue Ridge Mountains. The first meeting drew dozens of potential members. Thus was born the Transylvania Writers' Alliance (TWA), an organization that has persevered through many changes in circumstances and leadership.

In 2000, TWA published *Mountain Moods and Moments.* That book sold out at local bookstores and among friends and families of the members. Now, five years later, TWA is publishing *Out of Our Hearts and Minds*, a collection of prose, poetry, and drawings that reflects the diversity of talent in our community, Brevard, North Carolina.

Our title suggests the mystery of creativity; our writing literally comes from our minds, but it also comes from our hearts. The reader will find in this book work that inspires, saddens, uplifts, explains and reaches to the heart of the reader. We members of TWA hope you enjoy this book as much as we have enjoyed creating it.

Janet Benway,
on behalf of the
Transylvania Writers' Alliance,
Brevard, North Carolina

JANET BENWAY, our current Transylvania Writers' Alliance facilitator, is happily transplanted from Connecticut to Brevard, North Carolina, where she thrives, walks and writes, enjoying the mountains and a circle of creative, spiritually minded friends. A former editor and college English teacher, she has been published in such journals and magazines as *Lucidity, Bereavement,* and *Long River Run*. She occasionally teaches creative writing to adults at Brevard College and writes memoirs for people who want to preserve their life stories.

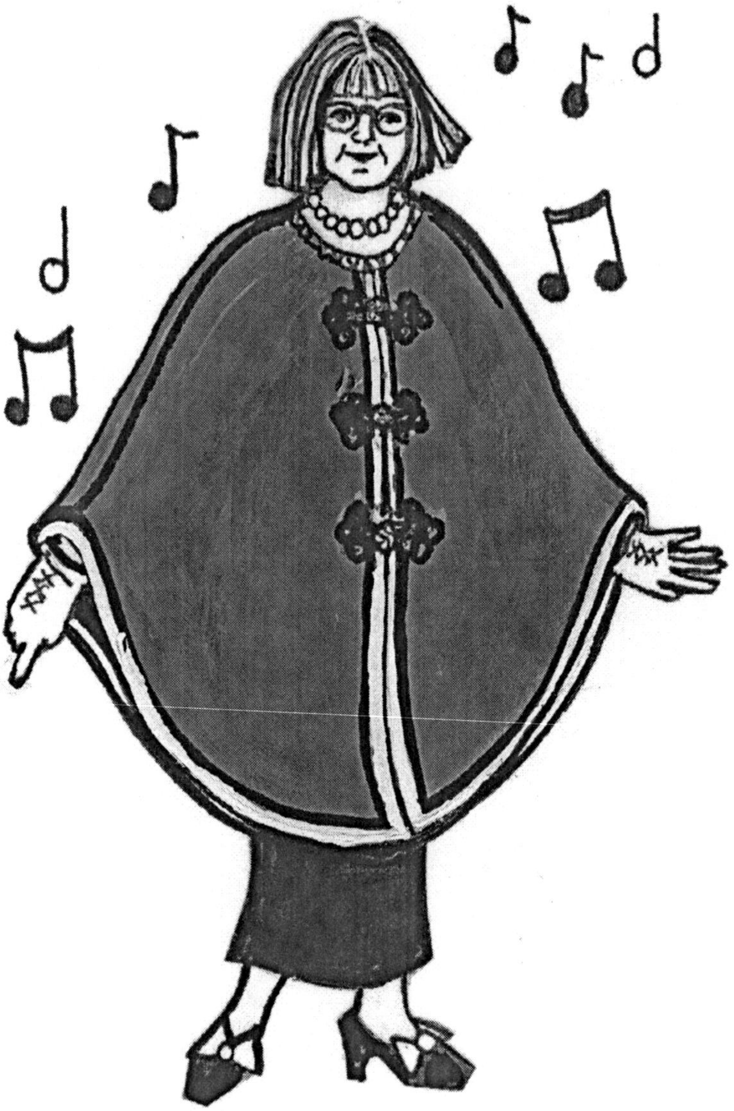

THE SCARLET OPERA CLOAK

In Memory of My Grandmother,
Sarah Alice Sloane Morse

My daughter asked me today
if I'd mind putting away
my scarlet opera cloak,
safe from moths and dust.
I must, I guess.
I live with her now,
and my room has just
a bed, a dresser,
and a tiny closet.
I had to sell my house on Francis Street,
my daughter's childhood home--
the beveled glass, the porch swing--
my cloak's one thing
I brought with me.
It's made of finest wool
with black embroidered frogs.
I bought it for the opera with
money from my job
as typist, clerk, and secretary--
tasks that took a toll,
but I was young and healthy
and didn't mind the role
of a woman in an office,
unwed, low-paid, but proud.
My cloak was a shroud
against New England's winter.
And when I finally wed,
that cloak came with me:
instead of attending the opera,
I learned to cook and clean,
though Elmore got me help:

Mrs. Murphy, who washed the clothes.
I did not like keeping house.
I wanted to read my books.
But I had to be so careful
about how my house looked.
No one knows the agony
I felt when my first child died.
I could not cry.
Five days old,
her baby skin gone cold
like alabaster.
Two healthy children came,
but their noise fatigued me.
I needed rest.
The doctors said I was depressed.
Those doctors do not understand.
They probe where they're not wanted.
I often feel haunted.
They ask me why I do not cry.
Well, tears are for the crowds.
I have taste and self-control.
Of that I'm proud.
I didn't even cry when Elmore
collapsed onto my dining room table,
dead before I could phone for help.
My best friend, Mrs. Ripple,
asked why I had no tears.
Even when my son, Roger, passed,
a man still young and bold,
my eyes remained dry,
though my daughter thought me cold.
She took me for treatment.
The doctors shocked my brain.
Sores remained on my head.
But my mood improved.
And now I live with my daughter.
She does her best to cheer me,

buys me pantsuits, bras, and slips,
but I like an old-style corset
to minimize my hips.
These brand-new styles
are not for ladies who are,
like me, well-bred.
I wear a dress and stockings
and high-stacked shoes instead.
My grandchildren come and go.
One day I decided to show
them my scarlet opera cloak.
They paid so little heed
that I didn't feel the need
to explain to them
how much I treasure it.
Slowly I cannot see the print in books;
my eyes are going blind,
and yet I find
a peace beyond age eighty
that my lot in life belies.
Perhaps I'm growing wise.
But today my daughter wants to put away
my scarlet opera cloak.
She cannot see the truth,
that it's an heirloom,
a treasure I bequeath,
a tribute to another time,
that underneath its elegance
beat a heart of young exuberance,
a feeling now long gone.
That scarlet opera cloak
filled my soul with song.

GRAMPY

A Tribute to My Grandfather,
Elmore Eugene Morse

Grampy may have come of age
in staid and stoic times;
Victorians were not known for risks
or forays into feeling.
Yet Grampy had a light in his eye
and a patience fate would test.
He loved my grandmother
with lifelong fervor,
she a beauty with snowy hair
pinned neatly in a bun.
He'd won her over several suitors.
Genteel she was and frail.
Ailing, she needed household help,
and he dried the dishes
after each night's meal,
watching time and pressure steal
her mind 'til doctors shocked her brain.
Painful as that was to watch,
his loyalty never wavered.
We, his grandchildren, savored
his kindness, his smile, his cheery mood.
Grampy's wit was food for thought.
His heart attack caught
us all by surprise.
Gram took his death with tearless eyes.
But we all mourned this man of love
whom we would treasure memories of.

CHAOS IN THE KINGDOM

I know I weigh three hundred pounds,
but I'm bound by inner cravings.
Food looks so good at the mall.
I was thin in high school, not heavy at all.
I almost didn't graduate,

flunked gym, you see.
I didn't want to change my clothes
and wear those silly gym uniforms.
Who knows why?
I cry these days for no reason.
My husband says I'm depressed.
I think my chest is too big.
Should I have breast reduction surgery?
But Dad treats me just the same as ever.
I'm his little princess.
We've always had a special bond.
I'm so fond of him.
I just wish he'd treat my mother well.
Personally, I think she lives in hell.
He leaves her often to go on trips,
and words of love never pass his lips.
I wonder why I can't bear a child.
I've been a good wife; I'm not cold or wild.
What is it that makes me ache?
What is it makes my mother take abuse?
Something ugly lurks in my dreams.
Life, it turns out, is not what it seems.
My dad can be cruel,
but not to me.
I'm his little princess,
don't you see?

LAMENT FROM THE LAKE

I don't know why it has to be me.
I love life too much to see it end.
But my father is the chief,
and I am Princess Pocotopaug,
and certain things are required.
The tribe is tired
of the plague. Dozens have died.

The medicine man has tried
his magic and his potions.
I've a notion to ask him
for a drink that will make me numb,
so I won't feel the water fill my lungs.
The site is prepared.
The day of the leap is near.
Dear to me are brothers three.
They will be safe, but not me.
My mother keeps a certain silence.
What is it that she thinks?
My father rules; we all submit.
Will he watch me die, just watch and sit?
I want the tribe's disease to heal,
so water will my last breath steal.
I'm ready now to face my fate,
but, Father, I face you with hate.

THE GRAVE OF THE UNKNOWN GRANDMOTHER

Who were you, Minnie Skay Muller?
Here you lie,
amidst black-eyed Susans
and a blue sky,
on a hill overlooking our lake.
For your sake,
I have searched for your stone,
but you are not alone
in your earthly bed;
your father and my mother
have names chiseled in dull, gray rock,
a block of granite, steely in the sun.
You were the one
who raised three children
as a lonely widow,

being paid a pittance for hard labor,
standing day after day during the Depression
in a factory line, ankles swelling
as you cast bells--
cow bells, church bells,
sleigh bells, tinkling bells,
haunting bells, reverent bells.
Your wages barely bought a house,
but somehow all your children went to college;
knowledge, you knew,
was the doorway out of the factory.
Your daughter, my Aunt Louise, tells me
you were timid, a gentle soul with quiet ways.
After lightning struck your home,
you gathered all your children in your bed
during every summer storm,
huddling together safe and warm.
Fears aside, you were a fearsome card player,
astute at bridge, a skill you bequeathed
to my father, your son.
A poem begun
at sterile graveside has fleshed out a woman I never knew.
I pray the words employed herein
have cast an image true.

LLAMA EYES

A Tribute to Rangika DeSilva, age 5,
Front-Page Photo,
The Christian Science Monitor, January 7, 2005

Girl child, you have llama eyes,
deeply brown and calf-like,
large in a face about five years old.
You are bold before the cameras,
your ragged dress

belying the dignity of your demeanor.
Behind you is rubble,
broken homes and twisted trees.
On my knees,
I pray for your well-being.
Some would sell you as a sex slave.
Some would whisk you to America.
Where--oh, where--will you be safe?
Strafed by raging waters,
your home is battered ground.
The peace that you embody
shows a grace that has no bounds.

CUTTING TO THE CHASE

This man I date is handsome
with a beard of snowy white,
a little overweight, but on the whole
attractive, a possible mate?

This man I date is educated,
a doctor with gifts to heal,
real talents to admire.
Do I aspire to wed?

This man I date can work with his hands,
forge wind chimes out of steel,
carve toys out of wood.
He's basically good, is he not?

This man I date is a veteran
who fought twice in bitter wars.
He has a sense of honor, answers duty's calls.
Should I overlook his flaws?

Then one day the neighbor's dog

wanders through the yard.
The eyes of the man I date
squint. What is this hardness?

"I'll shoot that hound," he threatens;
he keeps a cache of guns around.
I stop his hand; I plead for life,
knowing with utter clarity

that I cannot be his wife.

CATHERINE (KIT) TOWNSEND BORDEN was born in Charleston, South Carolina, but now lives with her husband, David, in Transylvania County with magnificent views of the mountains. However, Charleston and the sea hold a special place in her heart, as do the beauty and friendships she finds traveling in Mexico. She has taught all ages from preschoolers to adults, but young children are her favorites, and she has written a number of stories just for them.

14   Transylvania Writers' Alliance

HELP! HELP! THERE'S AN ELEPHANT IN MY SOUP!

"Mom, what is this on my plate? These green things look like wiggly worms."

"They're green beans, Zack, and potatoes with no gravy. You have crisp carrot, thin like chips, just the way you like them."

"But what is the green leafy stuff with the weeds sprouting in it and the white stuff on top?" Zack did not like to try new things. He was sure they might poison him and didn't even want them on his plate. Sometimes he thought his mother had pulled up weeds from the yard.

"Just try it, Zack. It's salad. Try just one bite!"

To get him to eat was always difficult. Usually his mother did not make him eat things he didn't like, but she encouraged him to try at least one bite. She loved Zack and wanted him to eat more things, so she asked others for advice.

The doctor checked Zack and told her, "He's healthy; he'll grow out of it."

His father said, "When he gets hungry, he'll eat."

His grandmother smiled and said, "He looks like a normal boy to me."

So his mother gave up on changes, except once in a while she would put something new on his plate. Sometimes he would try it, make a face, and leave it there and sometimes he would like it.

Now it was lunchtime, and he ran inside. He always ate the same sandwich made the same way; peanut butter on one side, jelly on the other and neatly cut in half. Sometimes he would eat a banana, but it had to be off the plate or at least not touching the sandwich.

But what was this? Today his mother had cut his sandwich into triangles! Nice neat triangles cut diagonally across the bread! He looked at his mother in surprise. Different! He did not like surprises on his plate.

"Mom! I can't eat these. The points will hurt my mouth!"

"Try them, Zack. They are the same sandwich, just cut differently."

He took a bite, a very small bite.

"Eat," said his mom.

"I can't," said Zack, "these are yucky, and I don't like them."

"Zack, you are too picky!"

But she took the three remaining triangles and gave them to baby Jeffie. He would eat anything, Zack thought. Jeffie would even eat alien food! He was too little to know any better. Zack watched as Jeffie ate the sandwiches. He loved sandwiches and soon had peanut butter everywhere. It was smeared on his highchair, his hands, his face and even his head. It made Zack laugh.

Soon his mother had made another sandwich: peanut butter on one side, jelly on the other, neatly cut down the middle with no crusts. Perfect! He ate each piece with delight. This was good.

The next day was a very busy day. Company was coming. Grandma would soon arrive, and his mother was cleaning, making beds and bringing flowers in from the yard. When lunchtime was near, his mother went to the cabinet to get the peanut butter. Jeffie was sitting on the floor, banging a pot with a wooden spoon.

Zack went outside to swing while his mother made lunch. When she called him for lunch, instead of a plate with a sandwich, there was a bowl with something liquid in it.

"Mom, what's this?"

"Zack, we are out of peanut butter. I was so busy getting ready I forgot to go to the store for more."

"But what is this?"

"It's a delicious soup. See, Jeffie likes it." And Jeffie was laughing and spooning up soup and spilling and having a wonderful time.

"Mom, Jeffie would eat mud pies!"

"Zack, there is no peanut butter. You will have to try the soup."

Zack stared at the soup. He took a long time to try the first taste. He ate a small bit of the hot liquid. It wasn't too bad, but it wasn't a sandwich. Then he saw pieces of pasta in the soup. It was a tiger or maybe a lion.

"Mom," he called, "this soup has wild animals in it!"

"Zack, those are like animal crackers, just in soup."

Then Zack saw the elephant; there was no mistake, it was an

elephant. Who could eat an elephant for lunch? He ran outside, out to the sidewalk. What a miserable day. No peanut butter and wild animals in his soup. His mother had forgotten him. He would run away and find somewhere else to live.

As he ran down the street, Mrs. Peabody called out, "Zack, what's wrong?"

"I had to leave. There's an elephant in my soup."

"An elephant in your soup! My goodness, is there a circus in town?" She ran in to call some friends. But Zack had gone.

He ran by some kids playing marbles.

"Stop, Zack, and play marbles with us."

He called back, "No, I'm running away. There's an elephant in my soup." All the children grabbed up the marbles and ran to Zack's house to see the elephant. But Zack ran on. He ran and ran until he bumped into Officer Pete.

"Why are you running so fast?" he asked Zack.

"My mom ran out of peanut butter, and there's an elephant in my soup."

"There's an elephant in your soup? We can't have that. We better call the zoo-keeper."

Zack was trying to explain to him about no peanut butter and the soup, but Officer Pete was too busy calling. Soon more policemen and zoo-keepers arrived. They were all talking so fast and loud that no one heard Zack at all. The zoo-keepers came with huge nets and tranquilizer guns, too.

As they were moving down closer to his house, Zack tried to tell them, "It was only a little elephant and maybe a zebra, and my mother is fine."

But they just said, "Did you hear? His mother is still in the house."

Zack shouted, "It was just soup, and Jeffie liked it, but I didn't."

But they all said, "Did you hear? His little brother is there, too!" So men with nets and tranquilizer guns crept closer to the house. His mother heard the noise and came out.

"What's going on?" she called.

"We came to rescue you from the elephant."

"Elephant?" she asked.

The children with their marbles were hopping about, trying to see what was happening. All the neighbors had come out to see what was going on, there on this usually quiet street. Mrs. Peabody was explaining that Zack had been attacked by wild animals who wanted his soup, but no one was listening to Zack.

The policeman was saying the zoo-keeper must have left a gate open. Other police were trying to keep the crowd back. The zoo-keepers were ready for anything.

Finally, Zack screamed again, almost crying, "It was just soup!"

His mother was trying to tell them there was no peanut butter, so she had made soup. They still didn't understand, so she led them into the house, where Jeffie was happily eating his soup: elephants, zebras and all. Zack didn't know what to say, so he just hung his head down.

Then his mother just said, "I guess everyone better come in for a taste of animal soup."

"Just soup, animal soup," laughed Mrs. Peabody. "Imagine that!"

"He just didn't like his soup," announced Officer Pete.

"Pasta elephants," chuckled the zoo-keepers with the nets. Nobody had really listened to Zack.

Laughing, everyone piled into the house for soup. Then Zack tried some. He had to admit, "Even if it isn't my usual sandwich, it isn't too bad to find an elephant in my soup."

From then on when people didn't listen, someone would chuckle and say,

"Remember Zack and the elephant soup."

ROADSIDE RUSH

The days pass by: sun, rain and breeze.
The cars pass by with seeming ease.
The destination, it is all.
We cannot stop to see what's small.
We do not take the time to see

The crawling ant or stinging bee.
But when we get where we must go,
We've missed the things that were too slow.
The tiny house with picket fence,
A museum now of past events,
Here I stopped with wiggly boys,
Tired of roadside, tired of toys.
A tiny piece of a tiny town,
Things people had and things they'd found.
The time we took was time well spent,
A slow-down time, no great event.
The destination is what's small.
We must slow down to see it all.

WILD THINGS

Yellow-headed stepchildren,
Persistent and wild, taking
Orders from no one, uninvited,
Each year appearing in the garden,
Blooming and sending out
Fluffy white balls of seeds
My children wish on.
Each year more numerous
Than the year before,
Bringing friends with you,
Filling the garden of neat green
With dots of yellow.
Our ancestors did not call you weeds.
You gave them wine, coffee, and greens
And they called you dandelions.

LIGHT IN THE DARK

We see a sparkle in the sky,
A tiny flash, a lone firefly.
He lights his light to find his love
From grass to bush, in air above.
At night it's hard to find a mate.
He blinks and blinks to get a date.
She sees his light and moves in near.
The glow gives notice love is here.
They linger, loving in the park.
Their love insures light in the dark.

BATTY

The little brown bats all came to stay.
We've used up all our tricks,
Noise and lights, but they won't go away,
And now we've taken our licks.

They have moved into the attic
And have had a brood of babies.
They give us lots of static.
Their bites may carry rabies.

Foresters tell us to wait a week
Until babies learn to fly.
Then hungry bats will leave to seek
Fresh bugs in dusky sky.

"Go up quick; turn on the lights.
Close up the tiniest holes."
They won't get in; bats will take flight.
They'll look for darker homes.

ORANGE AND PURPLE SUNSET

How does God find time each day
To paint the sky in bright array?
I'm traveling early morning roads
When the palette in the sky explodes.
It never ceases to amaze
To watch the sky become ablaze
As sunrise lifts o'er mountain haze
And colors come in streaks and rays.
It's times like these--cool, crisp, and clear--
I see his work, and God is near.

SPRING IN VERACRUZ

The fields of red flowers set my heart glowing.
Then next, a field of golden petals flowing.
On mountain rim are stalks of purple flowers
Glistening with the advent of spring showers.
Color where only brown grass decked the field;
The warm rain has brought forth life and left its seal.
Green pastures dotted with yellow buttercups,
The promise of life from death, come up.
Now the early birds, who come looking for meals,
Find tender shoots and worms rising in damp fields.

LIBRE

Wild things growing profusely by the road,
Nodding your heads with gay abandon
At passersby and visitors alike.
Color array unbridled and uncontained,
Overcoming less colorful weeds,
You return year after year,
Spilling forth to the very edge,

Ungardened in the proper ways.
Growing as you please, and please you do,
Cheering every passing traveler.
How I wish you would grow
So willingly in my garden.

HAIKU

Birds hop in damp field
Hear worms below, stop, eat meal.
Worm now becomes bird.

SOLACE

I went into the woods to see them.
Knowing they weren't there.
My heart was low; I needed them.
I hoped that they could hear.
Sitting, spoke my heart to them
Speaking of despair.
They listened and said nothing,
As I spoke into the air.
I railed, I sighed, I even cried,
Knowing they would care.
I spoke of all my troubles,
Letting down my hair,
Screaming to the world around,
Wishing they were near.
Then a ray of sun shone on their stone
That recorded their life here,
And remembering all the times we had
I thus shed all despair.

(In memory of Catherine and William Townsend,
St. Paul's in the Valley Cemetery,
Brevard, North Carolina)

AND SHE LAUGHED

"Caretakers of the world,
unite, revolt," I said.
She laughed, my mother,
Caretaker of my years.
She was dying, and she laughed.
"You need to put the tablemats
away at night," she had said.
She couldn't control the cancer,
So she worried about small things.
And she LAUGHED.

WOODLAND WALKS

Walking in the woods, my father stopped,
Stepped carefully over a small green plant,
Said, "That is a little brown jug."
He showed it to me with love,
Then trowel in hand, moved it carefully
From the beaten path to safe haven on the side.

THE WIGGLE-UNDER-THE-BED DAY

Sounds of running feet came up the stairs. The door flew open. Bamm!

A toe-headed boy slammed through the door, threw himself onto the floor and wriggled like a snake until he was completely under his parents' big bed.

"Billyyyy!" More running feet.

Puffing up the stairs came a red-headed fury. It was his aunt Eleanor, only a few years older but today left in charge of nieces and nephews who were not cooperating, especially this one. He had been throwing mud pies at his sister Jill in the back yard and one had landed on the clean drying sheets.

"And now, look at him," she shouted to Jill, who was looking like an angel but not doing much to catch the truant. "He's tracked mud all over the floor too." Jill didn't say a word; she just shrugged and didn't mention that their shoes had mud too.

"He just keeps wiggling out of reach. Jill, don't just stand there, do something. He's your younger brother."

Jill just shrugged her shoulders again and said firmly, "I can't do anything."

Running around to the other side, Eleanor tried to reach an arm or leg or even his hair to pull him out. She was very determined and angry. After several trips around the bed with no success, she finally stormed downstairs to the library, where she sat down to rest and think what to do next. Her younger sister Evelyn heard the commotion, came in, and said meekly, "Can I help you get the sheet down?"

"No, just leave it so Brother can see what his children have done!"

Evelyn quietly picked up some sewing and busied herself with handwork. She didn't want Eleanor mad at her.

The two children upstairs were giggling and Billy was out from under the bed.

"Billy, I think we had better do something about the sheet before Papa gets home. Let's see if Florence will help us." They sneaked down to the kitchen where they found Florence cooking shrimp gumbo for supper.

"Florence, we need a little help. One of Billy's mud bombs hit one of Eleanor's clean sheets. And she is hopping mad, but he escaped from her under the big bed."

"Lawd, chillun, you gonna to be the death of me." But she stopped what she was doing and went out into the yard with them. She was a kind soul and knew they meant no harm. "Why, we can fix that quick. It's only on the corner." So they helped her take the sheet down and Billy ran to get a bucket of clean water and a piece of soap. In a second Florence and Jill had it washed and put it back on the line. The mud was gone.

"Thanks, Florence, you're super. I'll catch you a little fish to take home for your supper." And Billy gave her a big hug around the neck before running to get his pole and find a few bait worms. Then he was gone. When Jill went back into the house, Eleanor saw her.

"Where's that rascal, Billy?"

"I don't know. Gone somewhere, I guess."

"Well, he better not get in the mud again. Just wait till I show your father the sheet."

Jill said nothing. She went over and got her handkerchief that her aunt Evelyn was teaching her to make with pretty embroidery in the corner, and began to sew on it.

Later when Papa and Mama came home, Eleanor had calmed down. "Brother, I washed my sheets today," and grabbing Jill by the arm, she said firmly, "Billy and Jill had a mud fight in the backyard. A big lump landed on my clean sheet. Then Billy ran and hid under the bed."

"What a scamp!" her brother said.

"And Jill was no help either," she cried, as she led them all out into the yard to see. They all stopped.

There was the sheet flowing in the wind, clean and white.

"Why, it looks good to me, Sister. Maybe you dreamed it."

Eleanor stormed into the house and up to her room. About this time Billy came home with two nice fish for Florence.

"Where have you been, son?"

"Just out to the battery to catch Florence a couple of fish to take home." And he ran to take them to Florence, who gave him a big hug.

They turned to Jill who was still standing there, "Jill...so, what do you know about this?"

She took a deep breath and told her papa, "It was an accident, Papa. And Florence helped us wash it and Billy caught her fish for supper to thank her."

"You two must behave when we leave you with Eleanor. And do something useful."

"I did, Papa." And she showed him the little handkerchief she was working on.

"Go get Billy and you both go up and apologize to your aunt. Off with you, now and I don't want to hear any more of this disobedience."

In the kitchen she found her brother, and Florence was boiling two crabs he caught also.

"These are for Eleanor, she likes them so. Do you think she will forgive me?"

"Maybe, when we go up and tell her we are sorry. Papa says we must." The two grabbed hands and ran up to tell their aunt they were sorry and would be more careful. The crabs would be a good surprise at supper.

BEGINNINGS

How does a sea creature know how?
Who teaches a scallop to furl?
Why does a sand dollar grow flat,
And conchs grow their homes in tight whirls?
Oysters and clams have dull colors
And coquinas grow rainbow arrays.
Wondrous things in the sea shore
Never ever cease to amaze.
When we go looking for seashells,
Do we wonder where it all began?
Creatures so different and intricate,
All taken for granted by man.

EBB TIDE

The ebb and flow of the ocean
Is much like that of our lives.
Each turn of the tide brings something
To be examined and judged,
Kept or thrown back.
Sometimes the water comes in force
And takes or reclaims things,
And we have no choice.
Take or leave, it is up to life forces
Over which we have no control.
Some tides bring flotsam
We do not want or need.
Searching and learning,
We use or discard,
Treasure and keep,
Or toss back to the sea.
Living means learning
To accept the ebb and flow.
For life changes with every tide.
It is something as certain
As the sun and the moon,
And the endless stars overhead.

ALEXANDRA BURROUGHS has enjoyed the excitement and beauty of the landscape and the people of Transylvania County for many years. When she retired from teaching English in South Florida, she made Pisgah Forest her home. *Bedtime Story and Other Poems,* published in 2004, is a collection of poems about her life in Florida. Now, if she's not writing at her table by the creek or working in her garden, she's in town participating in the vibrant cultural life of Brevard.

30   Transylvania Writers' Alliance

NOTES FROM MY WOODLAND GARDEN

What does it mean to live in a deciduous rainforest?
In a strange forest dripping with life,
Branches covered with lichen rain down.
Broken arrows that pierce the loamy forest floor
Remain upright interrupted in their downward plunge.
Messengers from the misty world up high remind me
While I scratch the soggy mulch, trim my rhododendron,
Arrange my ivy, dead head my day lilies,
That moisture permeates the pores of life above.
Lichen relaxes, extends her feathery tendrils,
Dances with her sisters 'til one night, one afternoon,
When strong winds come whistling
And rustling her curls and skirts
On her fine mountain home,
She plunges to my world below.

SEASONS CHANGE

Passion purple buried within a deep nest of knitted waxy leaves
Sprung open to translucent, succulent flesh
Suspended in a virgin womb of white adolescent fuzz,
Akebia becomes my tropical surprise.

Fluffy flakes begin to run up to me
As sun and blue sky refuse to surrender.
Snow showers turn my world to gray.

Puffball of a chickadee fences out the cold,
Perched, looking this way and that,
She pauses before dark and ice descend.

Crocuses, brave pioneers of spring,
show their sweet faces smiling up
from a chilly bed of winter brown.

THE BIRDMAN

Blood runs down wet shins and
Hands emerge from black neoprene,
The birdman holds the lobsters.
Vulnerable, cold night settles in
Matching tales of the hunt along a dark rock jetty.
In the glow of a warm kitchen
Ma Francis clatters pots upon the shelf:
Turns on the tap, fills one with water.
Soft voice, excited eyes describe
The fishes, crabs and even an octopus
You met in the wash of waves through
Jagged edges and slippery sides.
Nakedness, courage alone in a foreign world,
And gentleness draw me to you, curious man.
Tales of your hours perched on sand dunes
Watching least terns set and soar
Have heralded your approach.
Recording their comings and goings
From exposed nests upon the shore,
You track their breeding behavior,
Adding to our volumes on these smallest of sea birds
Who travel the furthest from pole to pole.
And now you track my every nerve
Tingling with delight.

MY HAVEN, MY NEST

I have a very special place
So right for every kind of case
Awake, asleep, reading or writing
Whatever the need, adjust the lighting.
Just the right softness, sink in,
Unbleached cotton sharp edges skinning.

Nuzzle, nap, enfolded; mother here
Each and every day of the year.
Watch the telly
On my back or on my belly.
With my spouse or with my silly
Self. Wrap a throw if it is chilly.
Books dispel ensuing boredom.
Champagne and truffles:
Can I afford them?
A little worn, a little messed
Punch up those pillows.
Who could guess
Relentless use,
I fear, will someday cause
Someone to pause
In judgment to remark
It's time to park
My blessed nest, my teddy bear
Some place quite very far from here.
I really should rotate my use
From end to end to cut abuse,
But it is very hard, you know,
When that one spot does make me glow.

MIDDLE-AGE SOY LATTE

It's difficult to open this waxy cardboard of soy latte.
Round plastic cap doesn't move at first, second, third try.
I change my purchase on the white disk,
Enlist the aid of the nutcracker and the rubber thingamajig;
Hold the angled container this way and that against my belly,
Too round right now. Must work on that.
It moves at last! Not impossible. Yet.
Now the plastic ring doesn't budge.
Pulling this way does nothing.
Ouch! Pulling that way hurts my shoulder.

All this before my coffee in the morning.
Before my olives, my mayonnaise and tuna,
My cranberry juice,
My Stoli, my triple sec, my tequila gold.
I've made my peace. "Isn't it charming," I say,
"To coyly ask my sweetheart for assistance?"
A smile, a look of the eye,
The proffered obstreperous lid,
"Dear, would you be so kind?"
Gone my proud independence
Hauling, carrying. "I'll do it myself, thank you very much."
"How long before it becomes impossible?" I ask myself.
Will I need assisted living just to open my bottles?
Perhaps a good neighbor will come by,
A sweet young man,
Or a sensible, civilized service,
My bottles and containers all in a row,
My meals and snacks planned accordingly.
How will I go?
Collapsing in the woods. That would be fine.
Wouldn't that be a fine way to go?
The beautiful woods, my woodland garden,
Ferns and flowers on the forest floor.
Pray it happens on a day that the gardener isn't coming
Or the sensible, civilized service.

I LOVE YOU, I LOVE YOU
(Inspired by Elizabeth Barrett Browning)

Just as the glossy redwing
And the little chickadee
Never tire singing
Their daily tunes thrilling with life
So you must never tire,
Beside our creek,
By candlelight,

Between my arms,
Upon my skin
Whispering those cherished words,
"I love you, I love you."

Oh, Babe, amidst the dark anxiety
Of a doubtful, yearning heart,
I cry, "Won't you please delight
In that most healing chant, 'I love you'?"

Mind, dear, that your words ring as silver-true
As Hopi turquoise rings or newly minted dollars.
False notes, out of tune, will toll the death knell
For a truly devoted, tender heart.

Who would castigate the stars
For their unknowable myriad dancing lights
Or upbraid daylilies for their countless brights
Adorning our winding, mountain roads?

So, dear, a daily paean to our love at sunrise
Will awaken my soul
In its lonely nocturnal sojourn,
Quickening life once again.

THE WINDOW SEAT

Daddy,
I cherish your eyes that looked
At the beauty of my mother,
Eyes that never strayed from
Your initial vision of her
On a window seat,
Hair aglow with background sun,
An angel incarnate.
You worshiped at her feet,

But she wanted something else.
She wanted you to win
In the world of men,
To outwit the competition,
To bring home the bacon.

TO JEAN, A POET'S POET

In your lavender pink suede suit,
A soft, blue scarf caressing your neck,
Frail wisp of a woman, you sit beside me.
Back straight and speech measured,
Mouth framing each syllable, you utter insights
Unimagined by younger minds
That rush hither and thither.
"The Depression? The 20's? Ask me, I know,"
You say, looking up.
My ear strains to hear the soft cadence
Hanging midair between each phrase:
Psychological insight, poetic intuition,
Girlish playfulness, womanly wiles
Tease my imagination with surprise and delight.
I teeter between offering you support
And genuflecting with reverence.
I shudder to think that I might step
On one of the roses in your garden.

YOU TRIMMED THE SAILS

Tossed upon the seas
Of loneliness and loss,
You trimmed the sails
And steered the course.
Forward we moved together.
Great storms we began to weather.

Batten the hatches!
Fasten the latches!
Warm lights aglow
Now wait below,
Fresh sheets beneath our quilts.
Tuck into love
(Forget the storm above.)
Tuck into cozy times
To cuddle and refine
The goodness and the laughter.
Tuck into ER
To Seinfeld, to CSI.
Tuck into cappuccino
To Courvoisier
To clarity and frankness
To vision and to kindness.
Tuck into love.

MY JAMES DEAN

My James Dean lived curbside on the sidewalks of New York,
Between services, among church-goers on Sunday afternoons:
A fisherman, perched to troll for a catch of pure virgin hearts
Spilling out from a red-carpeted, velvet-seated inner sanctum
Into the fine, wide way.
Deftly placing himself to advantage,
He worked his magic,
Surrounding, isolating,
Creating a surreal world
In a crowded gathering of parishioners
Circling about exchanging news of the week.
From the dull luster of a humdrum Sunday
He reeled in his catch to a pool of light
Vibrating with pulse and power
Demanding trust, adventure.
Once caught, they peeled out together,

Top down, to The Green or to Riverside
To sizzle on the flame of teenage hunger, incendiary.

YOUR FUZZY SWEATER

Tall, blond Swiss Graham Green,
You walk beside me along the Seine.
Your fuzzy sweater, forest green,
Worn from Left Bank angst,
Fills the space beside me, thrills me.
Your stride matches mine
Through alleyway, boulevards, parks,
Across bridges
To a bench between waters
You take me,
Green sweater warm around me.

DON'T CRUSH THE BUTTERFLY

Don't crush the butterfly!
Full spring sun after days of April rain
Propel us outside to the deck.
Coatless, even jacketless,
We sweep the husks
Left by our pairs of towhees, cardinals,
Chickadees and titmice
Trading places at the birdfeeder
Extracting the meat from the oilers.
It's Sunday. A day of rest.
Shall we leave it at that? No,
There's magic in the air.
Life is percolating up from the earth
Into our brilliant yellow forsythia and daffodils,
Into the ethereal ballet of weeping cherries
Waving their tulle blooms to the rhythm of spring winds.

White petals from Bradford pears ornament our cars,
Chase after us out the parking lot.
What shall we do to ride the wave of expanding life
Gently, tirelessly?
Perhaps a friend, a cup of tea, a tasty treat, music?
A friend who will enjoy the scene,
Rejoice in the beauty and
Share the magic.
Open the doors, prepare the place.

WALLACE GALLOWAY was born in his mother's home state of Florida, but like his father, he grew up in Brevard, graduating from Brevard High School in 1971, from Guilford College in Greensboro, North Carolina, in 1976 and from Yale Divinity School in 1982. He currently works in Congressman Charles Taylor's Asheville office trying to help veterans as well as those who are in the active-duty military, the National Guard and the Reserves. His deep interest in and meticulous research of American history are reflected in the excerpts this book contains.

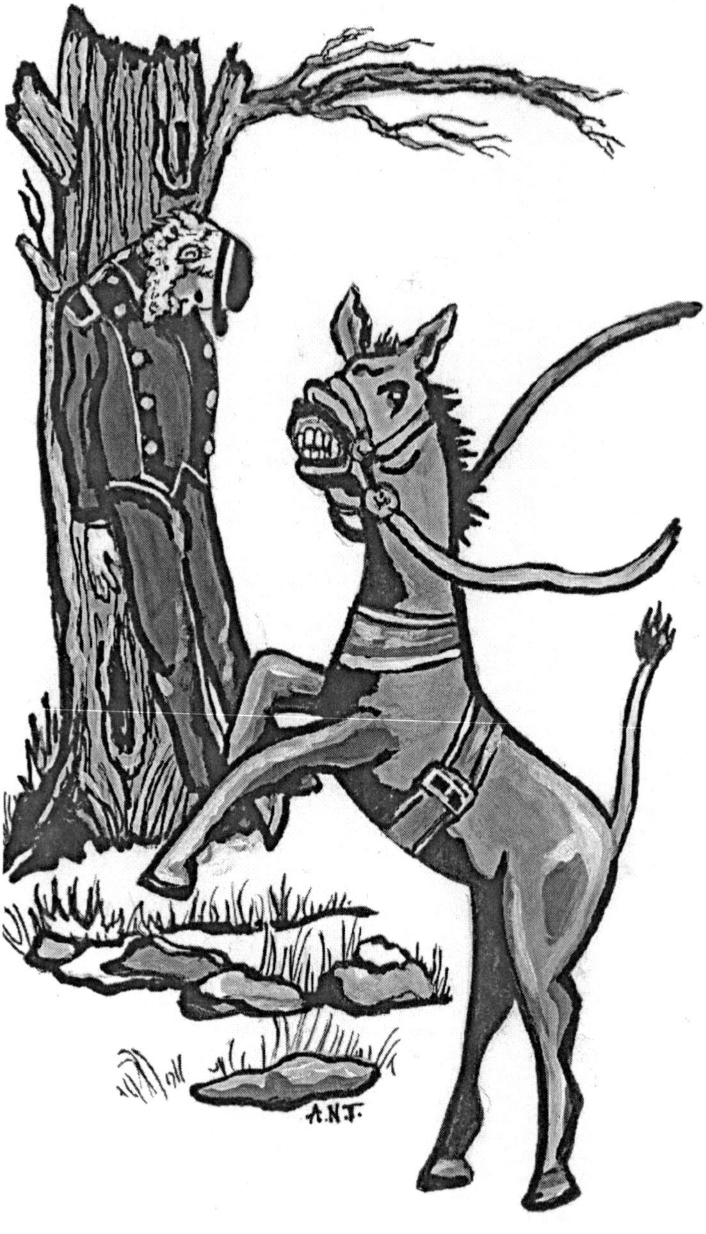
A.N.J.

AT CARNTON'S CEMETERY

These excerpts are from a poem of about 1600 lines called *At Carnton's Cemetery* organized into 18 chapters or cantos. The poem is based around the Civil War Battle of Franklin, Tennessee, that occurred on November 30, 1864, and events before and after it.

The first selection is Canto IX in the text and concerns the experiences of Hardin Figeurs, a 14-year-old year boy living in Franklin, on the morning of December 1, 1864, the morning after the battle.

The second selection, Canto XI in the text, deals with the reminiscences of Susan Tarleton of Mobile, Alabama, the fiancée of Confederate Major General Patrick Cleburne. Patrick Cleburne was born in Ireland in 1828 and emigrated to the United States in the early 1850's after having served as a corporal in the British Army in Ireland. He settled in Helena, Arkansas, where he practiced law. When Arkansas seceded from the Union in 1861, Cleburne joined the Confederate Army and rose rapidly through the ranks. At the Battle of Chattanooga on November 25, 1863, Cleburne and his division totally thwarted attacks led by William Tecumseh Sherman for several hours until the Confederate line on Missionary Ridge collapsed, and he was forced to withdraw.

After this crushing defeat of the Confederate Army of Tennessee, Cleburne's division was one of the few Confederate units still capable of organized resistance. Two days later at Ringgold Gap, Georgia, Cleburne's 4,000 troops held off 12,000 troops led by Union General Joseph Hooker for about five hours. This allowed thousands of Confederate troops and the Confederate supply column to escape. Historians believe that in this battle Cleburne saved the Confederate Army of Tennessee, or a large part of it, from destruction. On February 9, 1864, the Confederate Congress expressed a similar opinion by voting a special citation to Cleburne for his actions at the Battle of Ringgold Gap.

Though it was kept secret at the time, Cleburne's most famous action now is his proposal to free slaves in return for military service at a meeting of high-ranking Confederate officers in

Dalton, Georgia, on January 2, 1864. This proposal was rejected by Confederate President Davis, who ordered all copies of it destroyed. Fortunately for history one of Cleburne's subordinates disobeyed the order, and it became known when it was published in the *Official Records of the War of Rebellion* in 1896. Ironically, Davis proposed something similar on November 7, 1864, too late to alter the outcome of the war. It passed the Confederate Congress on March 13, 1865, and wounded Confederate officers and sergeants were seen drilling black soldiers in the streets of Richmond until the city fell on April 3, 1865. Cleburne's death at the Battle of Franklin is dealt with earlier in Cantos I-IV.

The third and last selection, Canto XV, concerns Confederate General John Bell Hood before and after his defeats at the Battles of Franklin and Nashville, his relationship with Rebecca Buchanan (Buck) Preston, plus some treatment of his post-war life. Hood attended West Point where he graduated near the bottom of his class. In the 1850's pre-war army he developed a reputation for drinking, gambling, and rashness. Hood suffered grievous wounds in the war and required morphine to control the pain, which may have affected his judgment. I believe he is a classic case of the "Peter Principle," someone promoted beyond his level of ability. As Canto XV contains a great deal of detail about Hood, I will limit my remarks about him here.

The name of the poem comes from "Carnton", a mansion just outside of Franklin owned by the McGavock family in 1864. Mrs. McGavock organized her home as a hospital after the battle and during the weeks afterward. In 1866 Mrs. McGavock organized an effort to disinter the dead of Hood's army from many scattered burial sites around Franklin and to reinter them on two acres of land on the McGavock estate. One-thousand-four-hundred-and-ninety-six of the approximately 1,750 Confederates killed at Franklin are buried in this cemetery.

I did not want to compose this poem in Whitmanesque free verse, but not being blessed with a gift for music nor with a great knowledge of verbal meter when I began my first draft in March 1997, and in particular not wanting to become entangled with the massive legacy of iambic and heroic pentameter left by Shakespeare,

Milton, and Donne, I chose to use a syllabic meter of eight syllables per line with allowance made to go down one syllable to seven syllables or up one syllable to nine syllables.

CANTO IX

Hardin Figeurs, a bright young lad,
Age fourteen, had been frustrated
That the war had gone far away
Where he couldn't see it, was now
Delighted that finally the war
Had come to Franklin. At first light
He was out of the house like a shot
But his exhilaration left
When just in front of his house
He found lying a dead Union
Drummer boy about his age,
His hands flung back over his head.
He had not counted on the
Tremendous racket of the
Battlefield, not that of gunfire,
But the noise rising afterwards:
The screams and cries of the wounded,
The neighing of horses and of mules,
The calls of the rescuers,
The cries of anguish and succor
Of thousands of human beings.
Hardin ran back to get his mule
And buggy hoping to find
Captain W. E. Cunningham,
A local Franklin man rumored
To have been wounded in the fighting,
But the mule, spooked by the racket
Bolted away dumping the buggy,
With Hardin inside, into a ditch.
Now a pedestrian, he was

Astounded by the sight of the
Locust Grove near the Carter House:
Six-inch trees felled, bark stripped from trees
Up to twelve feet, shredded tree stumps,
The ground seeming to have been
Worked over with a giant harrow,
All by musket fire. He was shocked
By the stacks of bodies he found
In the trenches. At the Carter House,
The bullet holes made the house and
Outbuildings appear to have come
Down with smallpox. In the yard
A dead federal was wedged standing
Against a tree. At the nearby
Parapet the heavy logs
Had been reduced to wood chips by
The impact of thousands of bullets.
He found a Confederate with
His jaw shot away, dreadful wound.
Hardin asked the man if he could
Do anything for him. The man
Had pencil and paper and scrawled,
"No, John B. Hood will be in New York
Before three weeks." Hardin had seen
Enough. He went to help his mother
Who was attending to as many
Wounded as she could. That did not
Trouble him as much. The horror
Was in a confined space, more
Manageable, where he felt he
Could do something to really help.

CANTO XI

In Mobile Susan was working
In her garden on a pleasant

Afternoon. There was a babble
Of voices in the street. It came
Nearer. Then she could hear the
Newsboy's cry, "Big battle near
Franklin, Tennessee! General
Cleburne killed! Many still missing!
Details of Mobile casualties!"
She fainted. She recovered--perhaps.
In October 1867
She married Captain Hugh L. Cole,
Soldier and lawyer of Mobile,
But died next year in June of an
"Effusion of the brain."
In August 1867
She told an inquisitive friend,
"No, it is by no means
An impertinent request. His going
Was terrible but his coming
Was terrible too, although, of course,
More pleasant, more delightful
But frightening also, very
Frightening. He was such a fine man,
The rare man who is what he
Seems to be. But at first I could
Not believe it and held him away.
On his second visit here he
Asked me to marry him; of course
That cost me many tears. That was in
February 1864.
Had I known it was the last time
I would ever see him I would
Have accepted at once. But I was
Restrained by prudence, afraid that
I was letting myself be swept
Away by longing for love,
Not love itself, afraid that I
Might hide from myself his failings

In my eagerness to find a
Husband. After that second visit
We never met again. We did
Maneuver for advantage in
October 1864,
Sought a chance to meet and marry
Once the Allatoona campaign
Had ended in the heartbreak
Of another near victory.
But General Hood would not grant
Leave, said he needed him for the
Preparations for the invasion
Of Tennessee. But we did keep
A mutual cannonade
Of letters from February
Until the end. It was painful
But comforting as well when letters
Came after I had learned in that
Dreadful way that he had died.
They were like final comforting
Words of solace from beyond the grave.
There was no good way to learn
The news I had so long dreaded.
But an official dispatch coming
By courier would have been much
Preferred to hearing the news
Hawked in the street. But to receive
That privilege I would have to
Have been a wife, and I was
Thwarted from that goal.
After his death I wanted to go
To Tennessee to visit his grave.
But my family was struggling
To survive; we could not afford
Such luxuries. But the harshness
Is now easing. Soon it may be
Possible. Hugh has encouraged

Me to go, laughed at my joke that
Such a trip would not have the most
Appropriate destination
For a honeymoon journey,
Said that just as widows and
Widowers can retain affection
For a former spouse even
When married to a second one,
So I could retain affection
For my late fiancé. Besides,
General Cleburne was a great
Man. He attributes his lack of
Jealousy to his being much
Younger than the General, more
My age, a man who had performed
His duty more subordinately.
And he truly does like the
Patina that accrues to him
From being linked to a woman
Once engaged to so great a man.
After our honeymoon when we
Have established ourselves here in
Mobile, he wants us to take the
Rebuilt railroad to Tennessee
To visit the grave. I so much
Look forward to marrying Hugh.
Different from Patrick, not quite
So stern a sense of duty. But
I am doubly blessed: another
Man who is what he seems to be.
Already those headaches, inner
Heralds of death's bitterness which were
So strong after Patrick died have eased,
And I emerge restored from the trough
Into which I was so deeply plunged."

CANTO XV

When the Army reached Tupelo,
Hood neglected to report to
Beauregard, to his great annoyance,
And the reports which he had sent
The War Department in Richmond
About recent events were so
Incomplete as to be misleading.
Northern papers had to be read
To get better information.
They indicated events far more
Calamitous than Hood had been
Reporting. Now truly angry
Beauregard, in Charleston, South
Carolina, decided he would
Go to Tupelo to find out
What happened and was happening.
He made the trip jolting over
Deteriorating rail track
In a car pulled by gasping engines,
(Detraining to cross Sherman's desert
And the Tensaw swamp near Mobile).
Shocked by the stark contrast between
Hood's dispatches downplaying losses
And the shriveled remnant of the
Army of Tennessee, he saw
Its men with little food and fear-
Haunted, exhausted faces. Rage
At being deceived turned to
Sympathy for the enormous
Humiliation Hood now bore.
He did not have to demand from Hood
A resignation. Beauregard's
Arrival being imminent,
Hood telegraphed Richmond to give
His resignation. Accepted

It was, along with orders
To come to Richmond and report.
It may have been disingenuous,
A scheme to keep himself in command,
By eliciting support through
Proffering resignation first.
But if so he was in a cloud,
Not understanding how eager
Davis now was to have him go.
Struggling to travel across the
Shattered South, he stopped at the
Preston family home in Yorkville,
South Carolina, to claim 'Buck'
Preston as his bride but found
Her reluctant. Perhaps because
When he came that February
He was not the South's young lion
But a mutilated failure
Now slinking toward Richmond
To receive chastisement. He was
Not the catch he once was, nor did
His wounds seem quite so romantic
As they once did. Indeed he'd changed
And often sat for long hours
Before the fire at a home where
He had become unwanted as
A relative, huge beads of sweat
Popping from his face, a haunted
Look revealing a soul more harrowed
Than any field at Franklin, the
Evidence of a shattered soul
Wholly thwarted, unable to
Wake from nightmare. He proceeded
To Richmond and reported, at last
Giving an account that faced up
To the disaster's breadth, but not
His own responsibility.

At the Preston's he had even
Brought himself to acknowledge,
"I have no one to blame but myself."
Now he blamed everyone else,
Anyone but himself. He left
In late March in disgrace just days
Before the city fell, Texas bound
On Lee's advice to try to find
Reinforcements in his own state.
Again he came, this time to Mary
Chesnut's home at Chester. (Mrs.
Chesnut's famous diary is
The source for most of what we know
About Buck and Hood.) From Buck
He was seeking some commitment.
He regarded it as a great
Exploit to have gone over to
To Yorkville through the barrage of
Preston family disapproval
And bring her back to Chester.
She appeared in public with him
When they went to the railroad station
To receive their President and his wife
As they fled south on his quixotic
Quest to find a bastion somewhere,
Perhaps beyond the Mississippi
Where he could continue to resist,
Detraining where the track ended
To transfer to horse and wagon.
But she made it clear she wasn't
Interested. He left, his hat raised,
Riding down the road from the house
As Buck watched from the window.
Days later Buck was spotted in
A carriage with "dashing" Captain
Rawlin Lowndes. On March 10,
1868, they married.

In another March in Richmond
1864, "Rawly" went
To a shop to buy some gray cloth
For a new dress uniform.
But they wouldn't give him the cloth
He wanted. It was set aside
For the uniform General
Hood would wear when he married.
All Richmond knew the rumored bride.
But Buck was not fully convinced
When he left to command a corps
In the Army of Tennessee.
That Spring, later to its command
And his precipitous slide
Downward to humiliation.
Buck bore Rawly three children,
Dying in 1880,
Not yet forty.
Hood pressed on cross country, even
With two young lieutenants it was
Difficult for a one-armed, one-
Legged man in a devastated
Land, in the twilight between
The collapse of Confederate
Authority and the resumption
Of Federal. Still unparoled
He struggled through the ravaged land
Until he reached the Mississippi.
But not being able to find
A means to cross, gave himself up
And was paroled at Natchez the last
Day of May. After the war Hood
Achieved a measure of happiness
And redemption, though still war-haunted,
Still fighting, but not the Yankees,
His former comrades instead, Joe
Johnson most especially,

Firing salvoes across book pages.
One comely cultured woman, Anna
Maria Hennen of New
Orleans, well educated
Prominent family, responded
Differently. She married Hood on
April 13, 1868,
Thirty-four days after Buck had wed,
Each wedding unknown to the other.
By her he had eleven children
Sometimes called "Hood's Brigade" by friends.
Before his marriage he became
An Episcopalian and
A regular church attender.
Tragedy struck a unit led
By Hood one last time in August,
1879, when yellow
Fever took his wife, his eldest
And youngest children, both daughters,
And himself. When doctors told him
There was little hope, he insisted
On receiving the Eucharist
Before he became delirious,
Closely following the liturgy.

JEAN HARRIS was born in St. Helens, Oregon, but her family moved to New York when she was five. She was educated in the City, and after graduating from the Feagin School of Dramatic Art, she appeared in several Broadway productions, among them "Brother Rat" and the Army Air Force show "Winged Victory". She also toured with Clare Tree Major's Children's Theatre production of "Cinderella". Thirty years of broadcasting in radio on "Aldrich Family", "March of Time", and many soap operas followed before her retirement, where she devotes her life to writing in the lovely city of Brevard.

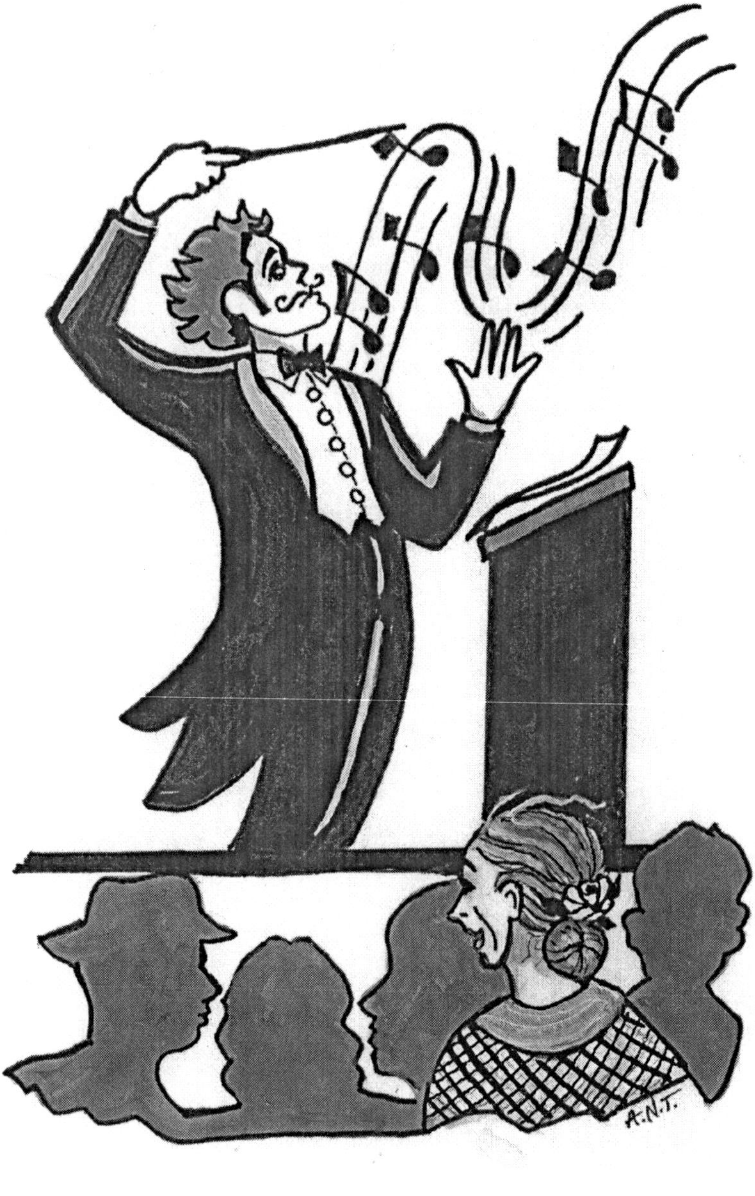
A.N.T.

STADIUM CONCERT

Miss Deitz had come to the concert alone, and now she sat in her blue dress waiting for the music to begin. Her pale hair was drawn in a close bun at the back of her neck, but one ash-colored strand formed a loop at the side where it had not yet succeeded in breaking away from the rest. The outdoor arena was filling rapidly, and Miss Deitz listened to the mingling of distant street noises with the steady hum of the people, and the sketchy and elusive fragments that came from the platform where the orchestra was already tuning up.

Miss Deitz liked to come to these concerts, liked to feel herself a part of this big compact unit, for when the music started, they were all one: orchestra and audience breathing and pulsing as one thing. A unit, and yet capable of being broken up into thousands of integral parts, each one a unit in itself and possessing an individuality apart from the others. It was quite wonderful to Miss Deitz, and she sat there listening to the opening movement of "Beethoven's First" with a feeling of peace and security.

The conductor and the men all looked cool in their white suits, but soon little beads of perspiration would begin to show along the temples, and they would lean into their instruments more and more from the excitement and exertion of the music. Miss Deitz knew it was hard work to make those notes come out and combine so effortlessly. So often the hardest work went into producing something which was meant to sound sparkling and spontaneous.

Miss Deitz recalled having studied piano as a little girl, and how her teacher used to tell her to practice a phrase until the notes fell away under her fingers like so many pearls on a string, none overlapping but just barely touching each other. Bach especially required that treatment. She was sorry now she hadn't practiced.

The second movement was beginning, after a slight pause in which the entire unit had hung suspended. They relaxed slightly as the Andante began, softly at first, and here and there bursting into a sudden and unexpected crescendo. Yet with all its surprises it had a lilting, haunting quality which always made Miss Deitz feel a certain way. It personified her impression of all symphonic music. It seemed to come at you in levels, vertically, as though you were standing in front of it, and it spread itself out before you; not evenly, like a carpet, but more like the ocean which sent one wave almost to your feet, and kept the next subdued in the background. It was made up of levels, which did not spread out like the ocean, but built up like a wall, a bright shining wall, which wasn't a wall either, because you could see through it, or it wasn't smooth and straight but changeable and unexpected in its symmetry. The orchestra played on, the contrasts in loud and soft very sharp, and heightening more than ever Miss Deitz's feelings about the symphony.

Next came the Menuetto, very gay, whole little groups of notes chasing each other and echoing back and forth. Almost mockingly at times, Miss Deitz thought, as she listened. This was almost her favorite of them all, and she nodded happily as the bright little notes danced after each other.

The opening notes of the last movement spun themselves on the air. Miss Deitz smiled to herself and moved her head knowingly as she recognized the interesting scale treatment, which characterized the Finale. Tantalizingly the thing moved forward a few notes and then stopped, exactly, Miss Deitz thought, as a lover might. A few notes more this time (one thought to reach the climax), yet the delicious holding back, the wonderful suspense as again the music stopped just short of fulfillment. Miss Deitz hardly breathed.

Suddenly, as if to take you off guard, the orchestra swung full tilt into the rollicking Finale. It was as though, now that they had held you spellbound, they sought to whirl you along on this abandoned accelerated tempo. As though they were making love to you, Miss Deitz thought strangely again; holding a little aloof at the beginning and purposefully letting go that aloofness a little at a time to heighten this moment when, resistance overcome, they could sweep you along on the swift current of the piece.

Only one thing irritated her, and the loose strand of hair looped down angrily and a little defiantly as she thought about it. That feeling she had had during the opening measures--that was all wrong. The music had made her feel as though a lover were gaily and lightheartedly about to kiss his love. That was what spoiled the music for her, and she sat almost resentfully determined not to be carried away or exalted by the triumphant sweeping beauty. It was not the lover's place to be tantalizing, Miss Deitz thought angrily. It was not right that the music should make you feel as though you were at the mercy of someone who could let you come quite close and then hold you at arm's length while you became breathless from the sheer joy and pain of it. That was the woman's place. She should be the flirtatious, provocative one.

Miss Deitz closed her eyes. She had forgotten the music, and her resentment at being carried along to the culmination of this turn-about courtship faded from her face, except for the little pulled-down lines at the corners of her mouth. She was thinking how strange men were that they could assume the prerogatives which so rightly belonged to women; how strange that they could do it and still have any respect. She hardly knew when the music stopped, as she sat there for a long time with her eyes closed.

RETROGRESSION

She scooped him up from the wet sand, loving the feel of him, and ran with him in her arms down the long stretch of lonely beach.

He crowed with delight, spinning the sound out, letting it be jounced out of him by the motion of her running, until both fell exhausted with the ecstasy of sound and motion. She lay on her back then, lifting him high above her, and he flailed the air with vigorous strokes as though he would keep his balance in this precarious new atmosphere, all the while gazing down at her like a small, jolly, and inscrutable Buddha.

She lowered him then and sat up in one swift motion, cradling him in her arms and pressing him to her. He lost his inscrutable look then and with round unblinking eyes appeared to be learning her by heart. He was utterly intent on her face so concentrated that she withheld her breath lest she intrude on him before he had found what he sought. And in that moment of held breath the universe itself was suspended for them, and they were held in the utter stillness of the present moment.

His mother returned quickly to the reality of him, but for the boy, for all of his life, it would be remembered as a nameless longing to return to a place once known. Or not known so much as experienced, as felt, and a strange restlessness possessed him as if he seemed to be listening to some high clear note beyond reach of the earth's vibrations.

He had indeed been lifted to great heights, and he must return to himself, reclaim his babyhood once more.

In the exhaustion of the long journey back, his eyes gradually closed, and he turned his face toward his fist. His thumb slipped into his mouth, and with a little sigh he abandoned himself to the comforting ritual of infancy.

EMILY

Everyone knows the story of Little Red Riding Hood, but did you know that her real name was Emily and that she had lovely red hair and a sprinkling of freckles across her nose?

How she wished that her hair was straight and brown like her sister Jane's. Then no one would pull her curls to see them bounce or call after her, "Hey there, Red," the way the big boys did on her way to school.

As for her freckles--she tried to scrub them off her nose. Her brother called her "freckle-face," which made her very cross. "My name is Emily," she said, "and don't you forget it!" She did not like to be called names. It made her very cross indeed.

Now there was a path near her house, where many flowers grew in early spring. She dearly loved the bright colors and sweet smells of the early blossoms. So one warm, spring day when the sunlight was dancing through the treetops, she skipped gaily along picking first one and then another of the pretty blooms.

Soon she met a fat Robin. He cocked his head and looked at her shiny red hair. "Ho ! Your hair is just the color of my breast. Do they call you Robin Red-Head?" Emily could feel herself getting cross. "My name is Emily," she said. "And don't you forget it!"

A little farther on she met a farmer. He was just pulling up some carrots to take to market. "Ho! Your pretty hair is almost the color of my carrots. Do they call you Carrot Top?" Now, she was really cross. "My name is Emily," she said. "And the next person who calls me names will be sorry for it."

Now you must know that her path lay beside a dark forest, and in that forest lived a Wolf. Everyone was afraid of him, because, although he tried to appear very friendly, he was really a wicked fellow.

When he saw Emily he thought to himself: "She will make a tasty morsel, and with that pretty red hair and those dear little freckles, I won't need pepper and salt to season her with." So he crept silently up to where she was busily picking flowers, and he fell into step beside her. Thinking to flatter her, he said: "What pretty flowers, my dear. They are almost the color of your lovely hair. In fact you look quite delicious."

"Mind your manners, Mr. Wolf. Don't you know it's not polite to make personal remarks?"

But the Wolf rolled his eyes and came so close she could feel his hot breath. "I think I will call you..." but he never had time to finish his sentence.

She stamped her foot and said, "MY NAME IS EMILY!" And with that she opened her mouth wide and swallowed the Wolf whole! Everyone was so happy the Wolf was gone that they gave her a big parade with balloons and a banner that said EMILY in huge letters. No one ever called her anything but Emily again.

A FRIENDLY GAME OF BRIDGE

I never did! I certainly didn't! Anyway if I couldn't play any better than you, I certainly wouldn't make remarks like that.... Well, I don't care! You had no business to bid that in the first place....No, you didn't! You certainly didn't!....I know, Jim, but listen! I gave you an informative bid. I bid hearts, and you changed it to no trump. If that wasn't bidding on a shoestring--especially when Alice bid spades, and you must have known I didn't have....Why we're not talking across the table. I'm just trying to show him he's not as smart as he thinks he is. He seems to think he's infallible or something. He makes just as many mistakes as anyone else. I get so sick of his jumping on me every time I do something he doesn't understand. You do, too, jump on me....You certainly do! All right, let's keep still then... I'm not enjoying this particularly. I know it's my play, Jim. YOU DON'T HAVE TO TELL ME! I like to think about what I want to play and not just throw down any old card....Oh, my goodness, I didn't mean to play that. Let me take it back! I get so mad at you sometimes, Jim! If you hadn't been nagging at me to play I wouldn't have done that....Why I would not! I suppose you never play a wrong card....It's always so much fun to play with you, darling....You make the game so pleasant....Alice, have you got your new curtains up yet? I was going to tell you I went into....Oh, is it my deal? I didn't realize it. Well, I went into that new shop, and I saw some just like yours, and I wondered....Oh dear, I must have dealt that wrong. How many do you have Alice? Six? Then I must have given you two. Silly me! I guess it's a misdeal. I'll have to deal over....What do you mean I can't talk and deal at the same time? I've even known you to make a misdeal....You oughtn't to have anything to say after some of the stupid things you've done tonight....Oh, Jim, you'll have to bid two of anything now, but for goodness sake don't make it....No, I'm not talking across the table. I just don't want him to make a mess of things like he....Oh, Jim, do we have to go over that again....I gave you an informative bid, but Alice bid spades, which meant that you....why that's ours....I trumped it! What are you so excited about....I trumped it. It's ours. I put my trump on that ace. Alice put the ace down....What? You put the ace down? Oh, Jim, I didn't know that....I thought Alice....Well, you don't need to have a fit....Haven't you ever made a mistake?

BEATRICE HEWSENIAN was born in the Bronx and mostly educated in New York City. She received an M.A. from Teachers College, Columbia University, and taught elementary school for 20 years before retiring to Brevard. Here, she and her husband have lived on a mountaintop for 12 years, soaking in the surrounding beauty, while she works on a memoir.

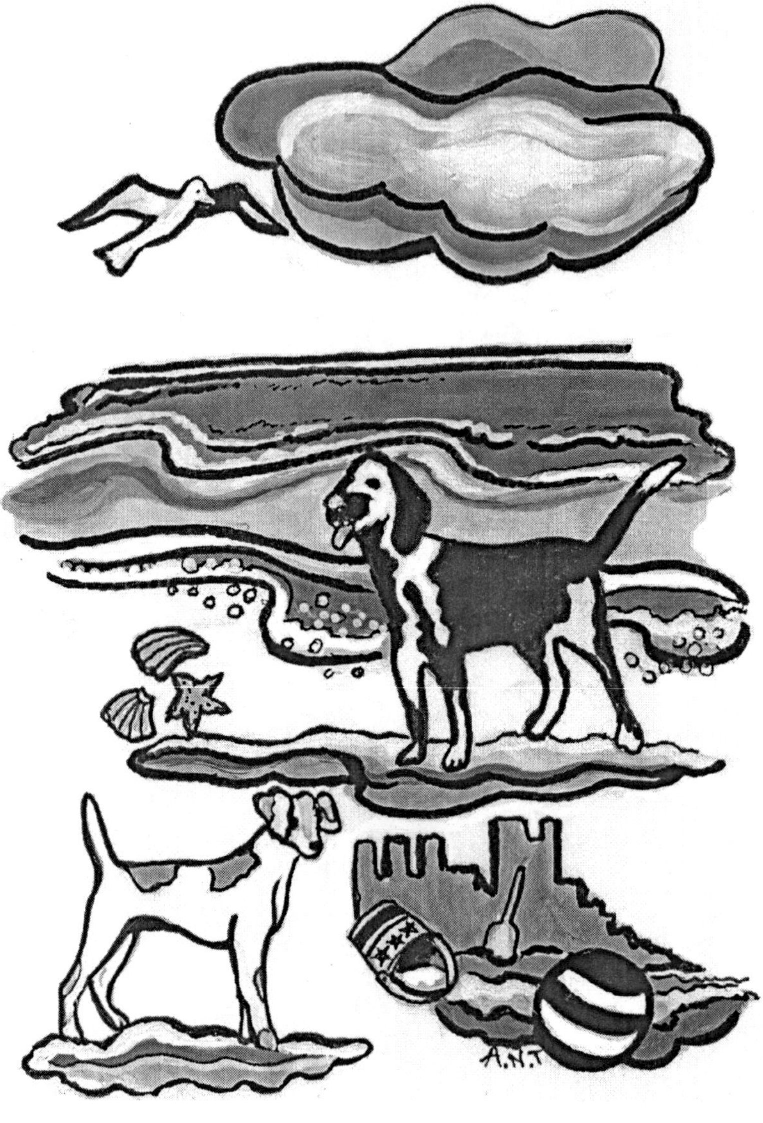
A.N.T

SAND

The wave comes to a gentle end
On the sand.
Some sand is swept away
Erosion is taking place
Like erosion in our lives
You know it's happening but
So slowly it's almost unnoticed.
No need to worry.
The sand is forgiving.
It is stepped on by people,
Pounded into pails by children,
Run on by dogs,
Used in cement to change
its personality.
Yet the sand is forgiving.
Can we be as the sand?

MEETING BOYS

    My girlfriends and I met a group of boys walking on Jerome Avenue. We knew that these boys had a habit of hanging around Schwellen's Delicatessen. We'd walk down the avenue hoping to run into them. When we did, we acted surprised. "Oh, hello, Joe, how are you?" We tried to act unconcerned, but at fifteen, sixteen years of age, we hadn't mastered sophistication yet. Sometimes the boys would ask us to go with them to the ice cream parlor. We'd accept. Walking there, subtly pairing off, each boy would position himself next to the girl of his choice. The ice cream parlor was at the opposite end of Jerome Avenue. Its gleaming white floors with small hexagonal tiles were set off by a black marble counter and high-back wooden stools. Booths lined the walls of the long room.
    One of the boys walked me across the park to my home on 205th Street. He kissed me good night on the outside steps to our

apartment building. I quickly ran upstairs. I began preparing for bed, getting into my cotton pajamas, pulling the white chenille spread back. Every Friday, Mama changed the linen. My bed felt crisp and fresh as I slid between the sheets. I could hear the Boy Scout troop disassembling over on Bainbridge Avenue. One of the scouts played taps; I could hear it plainly in my bedroom. As he continued to play, I looked up at the ceiling. Did I have a good time tonight at the ice cream parlor with Joe and the gang? I couldn't make up my mind. Then I reasoned that if it had been fun, I would have known it. Yet it was exciting, and I wanted to see Joe again.

"D" was giving a party. She called it a "bash." "Come to my bash," she said on the phone. She lived in a four-room apartment, similar to mine. I was intrigued. There would be some new boys present, as she went to Evander Childs High School, which was co-ed. Her father, mother and older sister would be gone. Kids were trusted to behave, no liquor was served, drugs were never present, and a curfew set. As we began arriving, we were told to put our coats and jackets in D's room, which she shared with her sister. Her parents' room was off limits.

We congregated in the large sunken living room. Music played on the phonograph, in vogue at that time. Some couples were dancing in the living room and in an attached foyer. Others milled about, chatting, eating small sandwiches and finger-foods in the kitchen. I knew most of the girls there. Again, I had mixed feelings-glad to be there, but unsure how I should act.

The bash had been in full swing for about two hours. Clare noticed that Penny was no longer around. Someone else said that Penny and Harold had gone into D's bedroom, where all the coats were, and hadn't come out. The word spread to the other girls. This was unusual behavior, and we began thinking that Penny was in that bedroom against her will. To believe that she had gone in willingly was unthinkable.

I knocked on the door, calling, "Penny? Penny? Are you all right?" No answer. I continued to knock, calling out, "Just tell me if you are okay!" No answer. Someone else took over with the same outcome. We stopped knocking and stood looking at each other. After fifteen minutes, Penny and Harold came out. Penny smiled and said, "Hi." Her face was all red. Harold had his jacket on, said good night quickly and left.

We dispersed into the other rooms, not talking. This was a time for thinking, and it was a revelation to me that Penny was a "fast" girl. In our group to engage in pre-marital sex was unheard of. Here was another part of growing up for me. I had been friendly with Penny, visited her house, shopped with her on a Saturday afternoon. This was a different side of Penny. It was not comfortable for me to think that she had gone all the way. She and I no longer sought out each other's company.

Going to Rockaway Beach each summer provided another venue for meeting boys. A group of girls would get together each evening and stroll on the boardwalk. We'd inevitably meet a group of boys and stop to chat. There was a lot of joking, laughing, and banter. We'd hang around for a while, giggling, and soon we'd say good-bye, continuing down the boardwalk, under the moon, the surf sounding, the juke boxes playing Vaughn Monroe's records.

Occasionally, one girl would leave our group and walk with a boy. This did not shock us, as we were somewhat more sophisticated now, but most of our activities were group-oriented. During the day we'd meet at the beach, everyone bringing a blanket or large towel to lie on, a cap, sun tan lotion, and lipstick. Lipstick was essential, especially if boys were also on the beach, scouting for girls.

Summers were enjoyable, mostly because I was out of school, and life was free. There was reading, which I always loved, and there was the thrill of the opposite sex, no matter how innocent. A boy might suddenly say "Hello!" as I was swimming in the water. It was a surprise, and my first reaction would be: "He's good looking! I wonder how I look in my cap?" We were all teenagers, growing up together in the years preceding World War II. Most boys did not have cars, but one group known by some of my girlfriends owned a jalopy together. One evening on the boardwalk, these boys invited us to an Italian restaurant that served pizza. I had heard about pizza, but had never tried it.

It was a big decision on the girls' part to get into a car with somewhat unknown boys. But we did. Going off the ramp, four girls and four boys, one boy began by saying: "The car doesn't look like much, but it runs." We proceeded to the car. It did look dilapidated. We were all standing beside the car waiting for the door to be opened, when, to our astonishment, one fellow lifted the side door off its hinges and said, "Pile in, girls!" When we were inside, he re-set the door on its hinges again and tied it to the post with a long leather strap. My heart beat fast as we took off.

It was only a short distance to the restaurant. The pizza came, and another girl who had never eaten pizza and I were scrutinizing the mozzarella cheese. How to handle cheese that kept melting and getting longer and longer, eluding our mouths? The boys had a good laugh! They took all of us back to the boardwalk and performed the same car door procedure. Gosh, I thought, I could never tell Mama and Papa about this life experience.

Another way of dating was for a boy to call up on the phone, the old-fashioned kind of rectangular, black, dial telephone, and ask to come over and take me to Krum's, the fancy ice cream parlor on the Concourse, off Fordham Road. We would, of course, walk to Krum's, talking, trying to be nonchalant and to act as if this was easy--something we did all the time with other partners. Once there, we'd go into the main entry, which was a large candy shop. Chocolates were sold there, and gift packaged and shipped all over the world, especially during World War II. Downstairs there were counters in U-shapes where ice-cream sodas and sundaes were sold.

A really heavy date on a Saturday night was to go to Lowe's Paradise theater on the Concourse, and then go to Krum's, across the Concourse. The Paradise had four thousand seats and first-run movies. It was patterned after a top Broadway movie house, although it did not have a stage show. It had moving fluffy clouds on its ceiling, stars that twinkled, large crystal chandeliers, and heavy use of gilded Rococo furniture and wall hangings.

My date for Saturday was Ed. He rang the bell at 7:30 and just stood in the hallway. I opened the door with anxiety, because this was my first formal date alone with a boy. It was obvious to me that Ed was even more anxious than I. He just stood there. He almost had to be pulled into the apartment. My father had already told me that he wanted to meet this boy. We walked into the living room, where my parents were trying to act naturally, although they looked like a tableau on a stage. I introduced them to Ed. Feeling the tension in the room, I announced that we had to leave. Ed and I made our escape.

Seated in Lowe's Paradise, I found it difficult to look at the movie, as I was sneaking peeks at Ed. He, in turn, was sneaking peeks at me. He reached for my hand and held it. I wondered if he would kiss me. Again, I wondered if it would be fun. Nothing happened.

NILSA VARGAS LOBDELL lives in a yellow house on four acres in a little valley nestled in Pisgah Forest filled with all kinds of flora and wildlife. Two visiting possums inspired her to write a delightful children's book, *The Story of Opie and Posey*, that can be found in area bookstores. She shares her home with an old tabby named Rocky. Among many of the things Nilsa enjoys doing besides writing is taking photographs, re-finishing furniture and making exciting finds in antique shops and thrift stores.

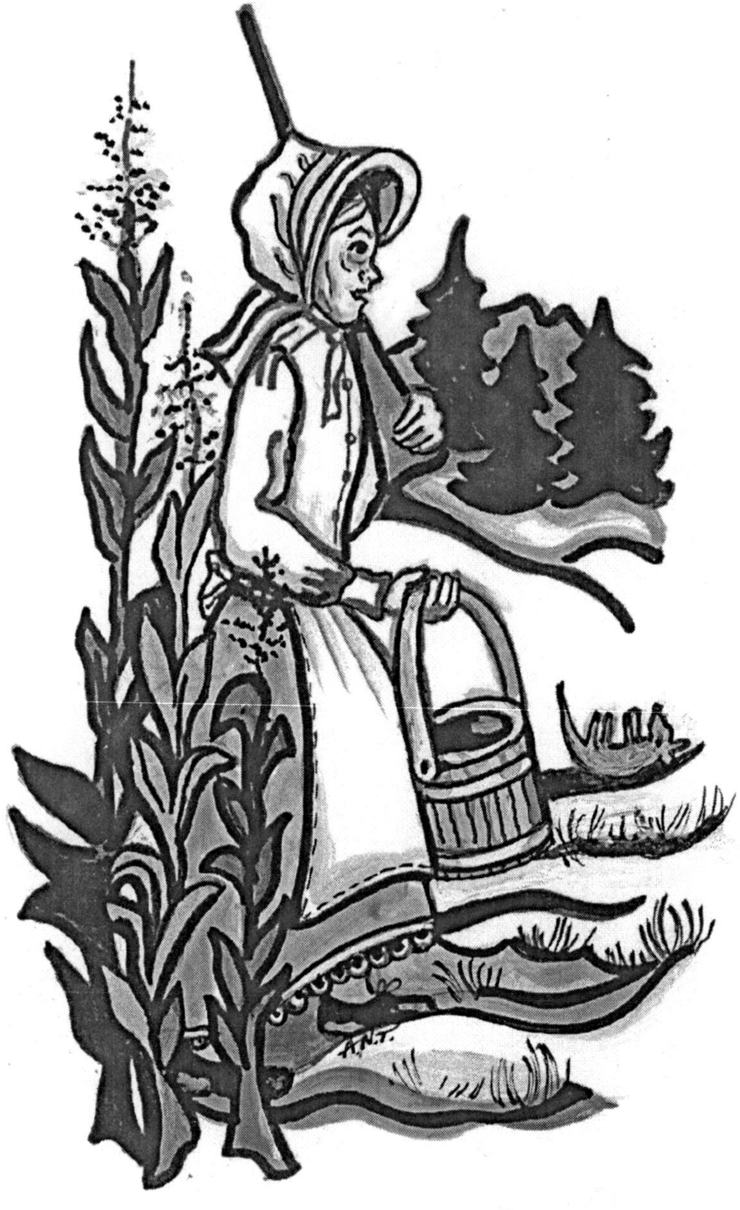

MOLLIE LYDAY McCALL

Meeting Mollie McCall wearing her old-fashioned cotton sunbonnet and ever-present clean cotton apron in her cornfield toting a bucket quickly showed me how out of shape I was. Mrs. McCall, an energetic 81-year-old mountain woman, put down her bucket to say hello. Feeling a surge of good will rising up in me, I offered to carry the bucket that she had swinging by her side. To my horror, the seemingly light bucket was loaded with fresh potatoes and large ears of field corn. Struggling to maintain my composure with my two arms solidly wrapped around the bucket, I staggered after Mollie. "What do you intend to do with the dried corn ears?" I gasped.

"Well, I like to make my own hominy. Make some up every year. I like to use 'Hickory Cane Corn'; it's a big white-grained corn. I scrape off the kernels when it's dry, put it into boiling water and add the dried corn. Then I get about half a gallon of green wood ashes, tied up in a sack for the lye. The corn is then boiled for a long time until the husks come off and the kernels are all swollen a big, fluffy white. When it all comes off good, you wash it and wash it and wash it some more and then you 'can' it. When you're ready to serve some, drain it, fry it in a little bacon grease and salt it. Add a little water if it's too dry. I do like hominy real well."

This then is Mollie Lyday McCall, born the 14th of June, 1898, in a little house back in the woods, up the mountain, up Turkey Creek. She was educated in a one-room schoolhouse in the old Turkey Creek Baptist Church building way long before the new one was built and moved to its present location.

Mother of eleven children, all born at home, she still has five children living. Strong, still interested in everything about her, she helps out her family wherever she is needed. Mollie has led a long, fulfilling life.

Her husband, Judd, worked in the forest cutting "Chestnut 'acid' wood," which was hauled out by teams of oxen and old wood-burning trains along the tracks which became the road into Pisgah National Forest.

The wood bark was taken to the mill, Carr Lumber Company, then in the little town of Pisgah Forest, and then to the Brevard Tannery Company, where it was ground into an extract called tannic acid, used in the tanning of hides. "Spruce Pine" bark made a chrome tan/blue-colored finish–like for sole leather.

Mollie often wound up cooking for the entire crew three times a day on a wood stove. When I asked her what she cooked up for breakfast, Mollie said, "I fried ham, made grits, eggs, biscuits, gravy and lots of hot coffee."

I asked how things were kept cool up in the woods before the days of refrigeration. Mrs. McCall replied, "Things were kept cold in a spring house or box. An actual box was placed in a running stream, which incidentally also kept things from freezing in the winter. A little house with shelves was sometimes constructed to keep butter and milk fresh. Hogs would be killed in winter. The meat would be placed in a box layered with salt and then covered with more salt and kept in the salt until summer. Then the meat would be washed off, dried and rubbed with a mixture of borax, sugar and black pepper, put back into a sack and hung."

Mollie still lives in the home she shared with her late husband built in the early twenties after the flood of Lake Toxaway swept away so many of the homes and people that lived in Pisgah Forest up Turkey Creek, and they had to move away. It is a cozy house next door to her son, close enough for her grandchildren to visit often. She keeps a large box of toys in her living room. She also has four hooks and ropes hanging from the ceiling on which rests her quilting frame. She lowers it down whenever she feels like stitching and strings it back up when she wants it out of her way. In the summer her back porch is a medley of blooming flowers, cactus and cherry tomatoes.

Taught to shoot well by her daddy as a child, Mollie still has a dead eye. This was proven to me the day I visited by the remains of a very dead rat mowed down by her old 22 rifle. The unfortunate critter had tried to eat some of her beloved chipmunk's food.

Sensitive, generous Mollie McCall always has a welcoming smile. She knits warm booties for all the children and lucky adults that come to visit. She has the old-fashioned grace to present a little child their very own little bitsy baby food jar filled with her homemade grape jelly. A precious gift of her time and love.

This story was written twenty-five years ago in 1979. Since then Mollie Lyday McCall has gone to be with her precious Lord, and her son Karl, the postman on our old route, has died. Her little house is still there, occupied by someone else. A small trailer park has sprung up in the field next door where her apple trees used to be. The Seventh Day Adventist Church is on the other field overlooking her house.

But not a day goes by when I pass her house that I do not think of her. I loved watching her braid my little girl's hair and wrapping a little length of thread to tie them off for lack of a ribbon. Dipping into her barrel for a scoop of her sulfured apples to send home with me. I am so blessed to have known this wonderful woman and hope that this little story brings some smiles and nods of "Yes, that was how it was."

Thank you . . . . . . Nilsa V. Lobdell.

THE SAGA OF THE RELUCTANT CAR

Stuck in the car.
Not moving.
Thunder rumbling in the hills
Thunder rumbling in the bellies of the children in the backseat of
    the car.
If I could move us out of here
Right now
I would undeniably move us out of here
Right now.
Sweet, smiley suggestions
from the rear.
Move the gear shift up and down.
Put it in reverse
Put it in forward
Try the key again
I try, and it clicks like the quiet snap

of a couple of fingers.
No thunder rumbling in this motor.
Raindrops are now splattering on the windshield
The car shakes and quivers as young bodies
thrash about in the rear.
"Can we go out?"
"I'm hungry"
"I need to go to the bathroom"
"Can we draw pictures back here?"
Pencils and papers are passed to the back.
Oh well, the radio works
Strauss waltzes blend in nicely with the raindrops.
The windows are fogging up inside the car,
Somewhat like my head.
Hallelujah, here comes help!
Freddie, the trusty VW, has come to the rescue.
And so has my son.
He attaches one end of a heavy chain to Freddie's
rear end.
The other hook gets attached to the front of
the reluctant car
Freddie pulls hard
I turn the key again
Thunder roars
Thunder roars in my motor
Thunder roars in my car.
We all rejoice
On the road again.

THE CHAIR

The chair was painted a scarlet red. So brave a color, so sad the chair. For the chair was a tiny chair, and someone had placed it in the corner of the room, facing the corner.

The tiny scarlet red chair could not see what went on in the house where it resided.

The only time the chair was used was when the child of the house misbehaved. So, not only was the chair sad at being placed in the corner, but when the child sat in its lap, the child would cry, howl, and wriggle its bottom unhappily.

One day, the person who kept the house clean accidentally left the chair in the middle of the living room!

What a wonderful time the tiny scarlet red chair had! It could see all around itself. It could see this incredibly beautiful room.

But best of all, when the child came home from school and saw the tiny scarlet red chair in the middle of the room, the child promptly sat down in it and began to watch the television. The child laughed and giggled and had a wonderful time.

This was so unusual that the mother of the child decided to leave the chair right where it was.

And so the tiny scarlet red chair and the child were happy.

LEAVING MOTHER

I stood there watching the nurse remove my mother's gold ball and pearl post earrings and then gently remove my mother's wedding band. She then turned to me and carefully laid them in my outstretched hand. As my hand slowly closed over the jewelry, I could feel that they were still warm from my mother. My mother stood there, a little befuddled and confused by the hustle and bustle of the nursing home in which she was now going to live.

My father had died five years ago from a sudden massive heart attack when I was 46 years old. It was a very hard time for me, for I'm an only child and was not expecting this loss at all. Twenty-five years later it still affects me when I talk about my father. I so loved him. He never yelled at me and accepted me the way I am, always so proud of whatever I did. Loved his grandsons and was totally taken with his two granddaughters. He was a lovely man: funny, sweet, loving. I still miss him so badly it hurts just to write this.

It was after his death that we discovered that my mother was suffering from Alzheimer's Disease, something that had recently become recognized as a disease after Rita Hayworth, the famous actress, had been diagnosed with Alzheimer's, and her caregiver daughter, Jasmine, had gone public with her mother's illness. My father had been taking care of my mother all this time with no clue as to what ailed her.

For a while my husband and I tried to keep her in her own home where all her familiar things were. I hired people to come in and watch over her. I called Meals on Wheels in Miami where she lived. The only hot meal they would bring was Cuban-style food. American-style food was brought frozen and had to be heated in the oven. I went ahead and ordered the food, but my husband discovered that she would put the food boxes in the freezer and not eat them. My husband would shop once a week and make her little cups of Jell-O and bring ready-cooked chicken and ham, trying to entice her to eat. She ate less and less and lost so much weight that her teeth became loose.

She continually locked herself out of the house so that the locksmith had to come and replace the lock several times. She would cash her Social Security check, go to the store and lay out the money at the checkout so that the cashier would take what was needed. People came and stole many of her things, and she didn't even realize what was happening. At last there came a point when she just could no longer live alone in her home.

I then brought my mother home to the mountains to live with my little girls and me. And so began a new saga of my mother's and my life. I became her primary caregiver. I bathed her, fed her, gave her vitamins, made sure she was dressed in clean clothes, and took her out for rides. She enjoyed the little girls at first, but then their constant being there began to tire her, and she would occasionally lash out at them and, of course, this would frighten the children.

Her faculties became less and less as time went on. She had gotten now to the point where she no longer spoke but was still physically active. She loved music and danced whenever she heard an old tune she knew. However, with two small children it was becoming increasingly hard for me to care for her, especially since she had now started to wander from home.

The straw that had broken the camel's back was the day that I had been folding clothes in the living room. I received a telephone call from my neighbor up the mountain on a little dirt road. "Your mother is here sitting in my front room. She can only say your name. Would you like me to bring her home?" I never even heard her leave! It was a very scary episode, and I was afraid that it was going to get worse. It was then that I called the local nursing home and asked if there was room for her, and the placement procedures began.

At first I had this wonderful feeling of the relief and freedom that I would experience from the constant care. Then when the nurse handed me her jewelry, all I felt was this terrible sorrow. My poor little mother stripped of all the things she loved. Her husband, gone. Her beloved house, her beautiful plants, gone. Her daughter now "getting rid of her"! And now this nurse removing her jewelry, especially her wedding band! It was all I could do not to break down and cry in front of her.

She was so confused; she was so small and fragile looking. A little wisp of a person, left among strangers, in a strange place. I knew this was the best thing to do, but still it was so hard. My mother. "For heaven's sake, it's my mother!" Lord, how could this happen! You are not supposed to leave your mother. I felt so guilty. Even now after so many years, I still feel guilty. Could I have done more? Why did I put my children first? Shouldn't I have put my mother first? I was so tired.

My mother lived another five years in the nursing home. For, of course, they gave her excellent care. I visited every day and brought the children to see her. I made sure she had nice clothes to wear, brought her a little TV and her favorite potted plant of African violets. I had her doctor put a "No Heroics" on her chart. I consulted with the funeral home across the street. Everything was ready.

Christmas weekend we went in to sing to her and wish her well. We didn't know if she could hear or understand us, as she had been bed-ridden for a while now, curled up in a fetal position. They say you never know what is going on in a person's head, so we went on with our cheery songs. After that we went on our annual trip to Florida and while we were gone, my mother left us.

It's strange. No matter how much a person is prepared, and

goodness knows I was well prepared, when death came to my mother, I really was not so prepared. I mourn her still. I wish she were here to see her grandchildren grown and beautiful. She would be so proud of them. Her great-granddaughters and now another one on the way would have thrilled her. She could have taught them so much.

    I leave you now, Mom. Love, from your daughter.

MARILYN OPALOYD ONG lives in Brevard with her husband and several cats where she runs the Red House Bed and Breakfast.

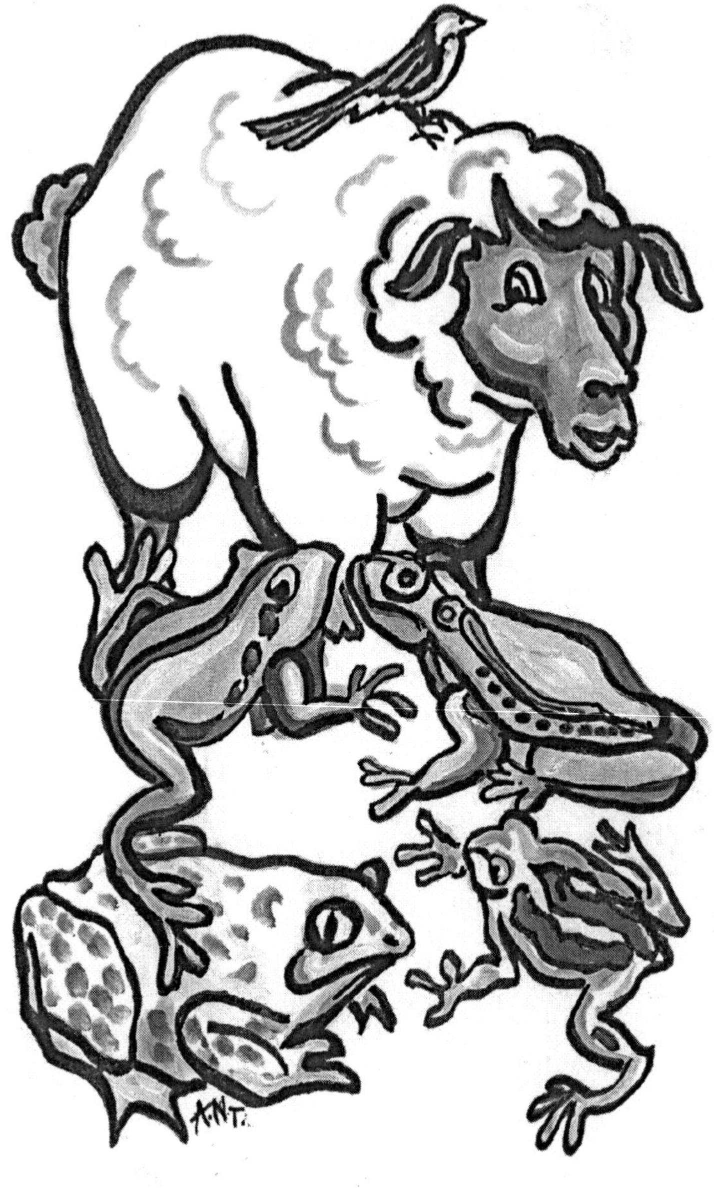
A.N.T.

ARIZONA MURPHY

When I was a little girl, the only folks who were sent off to the Homes for the Aged came from either very poor families or very rich ones. Fortunately, ours was neither, so my grandmother, Arizona Murphy, lived with us. She slept in a bed under the window in my room, and everyone praised me for my unselfishness over the arrangement. The truth was, I loved having her in my room with me. At night, when the whole flat was dark, and everyone else already in bed and asleep, she'd come and sit on my bed cross-legged like a guru, before gurus were fashionable, and tell me stories, mostly ghost and fairy stories, about her days as a young girl in the South of Ireland in the mist-filled areas of the mountains of the high country. She'd tell me about her pet lamb she'd smuggled into her room at night, about the frogs she brought into the house in the winter and made them little jackets and about the bluebirds that flew into her room to eat. Houses in Ireland didn't have screens, so if she opened the window the birds flew in, particularly since she put birdseed on the dresser under the window just inside the room.

Her stories never really scared me, but to make her happy I'd shudder and groan a lot. If I got too noisy she'd put her hand over my mouth lest my aunt Ola came padding down the narrow corridor in her maroon felt house slippers to hush us up. Her slippers flipped and flapped on the floor so we could always hear her coming, something she never did figure out.

After Grandmother Arizona came to live with us, I stopped being so lonely, and my imaginary friends had to find new friends to play with. We hung around together, although the neighbors and, of course, some of the family thought it wasn't right even though my aunt and uncle, with whom we lived, didn't fuss. I'm sure they were glad to have both of us occupied and out of their hair.

Thursday was Grandma's day in the kitchen. Before she came, my father had worked out an elaborate plan on a paper that was taped up in the hall. This was so that things would go smoothly between his sister and his mother. Thursdays in the kitchen was part of this plan. This enabled Aunt Ola to get out of the house in the afternoon, and I'd get to stay with Grandma in the kitchen.

Sometimes we'd make pecan fudge for my daddy, or sugar cookies for everyone or cupcakes for Grandma's sewing club, but the best of all was when we made chicken soup. I say "we" with truth because Grandma believed that learning was doing. Not like Aunt Ola. She would let me watch or bring her things like the salt or the flour, and if she was in a particularly good mood she would let me stir, but Grandma let me do everything by myself. She would lean against the counter and read the recipe out loud while I followed what she said with the skill of a nine-year-old chef. Although I spilled things and broke a couple of dishes, I never got burned or scorched a pot. Still, my cooking was something we never mentioned to Aunt Ola.

One of the reasons I liked chicken-soup Thursday so much was because the chicken soup wasn't for home. When it was finished, Grandma would pour it into big old green glass mason jars and let it cool. Then she'd put it into a big wicker basket with a handle, and we'd go visit with the heavy basket over her arm. Over the years Grandma Arizona had acquired an amazing bunch of friends. Quite an assortment, the kind of folks she could never have invited into Aunt Ola's home, let alone let her know she even knew such people. There was Hannah Crome, a retired exotic dancer. She lived over an awful, sour-smelling tavern in a small yellow room with vases of dirty plastic roses everywhere. She got to live in this room because she cleaned up the sour-smelling pub after it closed in the middle of the night. Her clothes looked like old costumes with sequins and fringe strategically placed to camouflage the moth holes and grease stains. Hannah weighed well over 200 pounds, and to my eyes it was hard to see how she had ever really danced very well, but maybe dancing was not the real talent needed for an exotic dancer. In those days I wasn't quite sure what an exotic dancer was.

Hannah would get out three mismatched bowls and spoons and a plate of crackers. She made slurping sounds as she ate, and I knew that Aunt Ola would never have eaten a meal with her, slurping annoyed Aunt Ola terribly. But Grandma and I didn't mind. The best part of eating with Hannah was that after we ate she would heave herself out of her chair and go to a metal cabinet and come back with this gooey pink candy. The stuff stuck to the roof of my mouth, but back then we didn't have sugar so anything sweet was worth the trouble. Sometimes she had beer in her window box, and she gave a bottle to Grandma and a tiny glass to me. We added that to the list of things we didn't tell Aunt Ola about.

Another recipient of our chicken soup was Mr. Furry, a pleasant old junk dealer with the black Irish look about him, lots of bushy salt-and-pepper hair and a dark forbidding mustache. He owned a big shabby place with a high fence around it in the business district. His junk was displayed in the front high-ceilinged rooms with water stains on the wallpaper that widened after each bad rain from the leaky roof. When we came by, he put the "closed" sign on the door and took us into the back where he had his quarters.

Grandma and he had known each other all their lives, and they giggled over the latest gossip while I roamed all over the top stories of the house through the dusty, furniture-stuffed rooms. I peeked into the closets and furniture as only a bored nine-year-old can do and convinced myself that someday I would find a body or, better yet, a big bag of money in one of the old closets or trunks. For the record, I never did because there was absolutely nothing sinister about Mr. Furry. He was warm and open; it was really just all those American Nancy Drew mysteries that I was reading that gave me those ideas. Nancy Drew was always finding something hidden.

On the landing of the second floor there was a massive piano that I used to try to play. It was seriously out of tune with the old keys chipped and yellowed. The piano had an old scarf with long fringe on it on top of it, and I would pull it off and wrap it around me and act like a tango dancer all alone up there by myself. As I was replacing the scarf one day, I noticed that the top was hinged and could be lifted. It was a wonder the keys had moved at all, because lying neatly on the strings inside the lid were lots of bottles of whiskey and red wine. When I told my grandmother, she just crinkled up her eyes, gave me a wink and reminded me not to tell my aunt Ola.

I think, as I look back, that Mr. Furry was my favorite of all of Grandma's friends because he made my grandmother blush and look so pretty under his fond eyes. To him she had never gotten old but was instead the same girl he had known fifty years ago. He also slipped me some coins when we left so we could stop by the bakery or candy store on our way back home and buy something we could stuff ourselves with before we got there.

Mrs. Higgins on Front Street also got chicken soup. She had a flat on a dismal street on an awful river where boats blew mournful whistles that penetrated her wall all day. She had a ragged, dirty, old couch where we all sat in a row because that was the only place to sit. She would moan about how awful her life was, and Grandma would pat her on the arm and tell her better times were coming, although, even to my nine-year-old ears, I knew she wasn't telling the truth.

Eddie lived near the river too. He had no last name that I ever heard and was the whitest person I had ever seen. Grandma told me I had to be quiet around Eddie, because he was dying. He was young, even younger than my father, and in those days I thought you had to be old to die. Grandma fed him with a spoon and bathed his face and cleaned up his room and his kitchen. Freddie would tremble and shake and cry, and Grandma would tell me to go sit on the front steps. It always seemed to be such a long time until she came out, and I could see she was squeezing the tears back behind her eyes.

Sometimes our last stop was at Miss Cinders' big fine brick house. She had dark shiny furniture, crystal lamps, red-velvet drapes, dark-blue printed carpeting and a small terrier dog that I hated because he'd bark and sniff at us the whole time we were there. I tried awfully hard to like Miss Cinders, but it never worked. I was curious why we had to visit that house, because to my mind she was just about as rich as anyone could get. When I got around to asking about this, Grandma said, "Just because a person has money doesn't mean they have stopped needing people."

The visits over for the day, we would start home. My aunts would be sitting on the porch if the weather was nice, and Grandma would just go on into the house, leaving me there to answer their questions about the day. She knew I could be trusted to leave the right things out of my report. I never told that we went to see a dying man, because they would have made us boil our clothes and take strong lye soap baths in steaming water. And I never told them about Hannah's immense cleavage and her funny clothes or the beer she gave me to drink or about the serious talk she gave me telling me about life. The main thing I remember about this talk was that she told me that as I got older it was imperative that my husbands get younger. And I never told my aunts about Mr. Furry and Grandma giggling downstairs, while I was upstairs rummaging through his things.

When I think of a good person, I compare them to my grandmother, Arizona Murphy. I loved her more than anyone else in my growing-up world, and I absolutely knew she loved me best, and at night after my prayers, when my Aunt Ola asked me whom I loved best, I always said God and Jesus, because I knew that was what she wanted to hear, but under my breath I quietly whispered, "Grandma Arizona." I knew there was no doubt that God and Jesus would understand.

A GIFT OF KNOWLEDGE

Mary Beth was born an Irish Catholic girl. She knew the right things to do and how to be properly guilty if she didn't do them.

She grew up with practical 1950's parents, a mother who always washed her aluminum foil after she used it and stored it away to reuse it later until it got holes in it, and a father who was happier getting his old shoes re-soled than buying new ones. Her parents always fixed up and kept things that they might need or could reuse later.

All that fixing up and re-doing just drove her crazy. Just once she wanted to be wasteful and discard something simply because she wanted to have something different, not waiting to throw it away only because it was beyond salvaging.

And then she discovered that sometimes, when you throw things away, they can be replaced by something new, different, less boring and infinitely more exciting.

After a disastrous affair, which left her with one pair of shoes, two sweaters, a raincoat, three socks, and a bad cold, she decided she needed a plan for her personal life that would include her new way of thinking. She wanted her men to be like her garden, colorful every minute with absolutely no perennials to be around next year and no new baby plants that would need extra care. What she wanted was annuals, the kind of plants that delivered quickly, in a short time, and were wonderful to look at and enjoy while they were doing so.

So, she soon found that it was easier to have different men for the different seasons instead of expecting one man alone to be sufficient for the whole year. It was easier on her and certainly less confusing for the men. After she figured out the plan, she decided she had been given a great gift of knowledge and that she needed to use it to its full potential, fearful that unless she used it well it would be passed on to some other needy woman. A gift just for herself, something special she had been wanting her whole life, because it could be a great secret that would make her life much more pleasant and keep it running more comfortably.

The winter man never made it through to spring. There was something about a man who loved heavy foods, drank whiskey, built good wood fires, wore tweeds, smoked a pipe and who loved to sit and read as well as play in the snow. A man who was rather soft to cuddle with because he had no desire to go out running in the early morning hours through the icy streets just for his health. But, he was not someone she could envision eating sweet cake with and drinking mint tea with outside in the springtime garden.

Springtime men wanted for new things. They had young-time energy. With all the windows open as well as the doors and the smell of fresh mown grass instead of wood smoke in the air, they were off to search for rowboat oars and fishing gear. Spring brought new and improved and generally younger men who recognized her more as an equal instead of a mother or a soul mate companion. They looked upon life as a tire swing hung in a tree. And if they swung too high and fell out, they just climbed back on and tried to go higher the next time. Big shaggy dogs and pussy cats adored them, and big wicker picnic baskets with fried chicken and ripe melons were part of their gear. They were always looking for a new shady spot to do nothing but idle away the afternoon with a chilled bottle of wine where no one could find them.

The summer brought men who looked good in shorts and tank tops as they climbed on their motorcycles, somebody she could eat a bowl of cherries with and spit the pits off the porch while the dogwoods and azaleas exploded around them in a riot of color. Someone who brought with him that feeling that anyone could accomplish anything and do anything and, best of all, at anytime at all. And if the laze of a summer afternoon overtook this wild ambition, then that was all right too. Summer needed a man who would sit in a rocker on a porch on a hot August day just because it was cooler there. A man who, when the evening cooled, bought her a big floppy hat and took her for a ride on a side road in his car with the top down just because the evening was so lovely.

The autumn man tended toward substance. With the holiday season nearing, it was time to look for a little security and dignity in the shimmer of someone flashier. Simplicity in a person could be a very exciting quality. It was surprising how few people realized this, particularly after a busy winter, spring and summer. A slow-moving man in the fall was a comfort and gave one time to plan ahead for the spring and summer. The fall man needed to look good in a tuxedo and like to dance, particularly with the New Year's coming at the end of his reign. The fall man needed to be quite presentable. Because so many family affairs occur around the holidays, he had to have good manners and know his way around the linens and silver on the dining table. This had to be a more serious man, a more intelligent man, one necessary to the season. This time of the year needed a man who felt that laughing was as necessary as breathing and that if you didn't do something when you came to it, you may never come to it to do it again.

And as the year came to an end, there were the delicious thoughts of what could be ahead in the winter, spring, and summer of the next year. Wonderful dreams eased one along through those long, dark winter nights, knowing that the springtime nights with their balmy winds were next....

A TRUE STORY

This is mostly a true story. It is one of the few things my husband and I do together. We have done it together several times a year ever since we have been married and in many parts of the United States. Now everyone says, "What is wrong with you two? With your old bones you shouldn't be doing anything so risky." But it's like riding a motorcycle ninety miles an hour up into the forest; it cuts down on the boredom of our everyday life. My neighbor Elizabeth used to say that she lived two lives, her real everyday life and then the world she escaped into so she could stand her everyday life.

We go up to Tennessee to run the whitewater rapids back down to the French Broad River to near Asheville, a serious whitewater challenge. Since I never learned to swim, it makes it an even more thrilling adventure for me. It is a four- or five-day trip, and we have done it so much we know what to take on the river and what not to take. Along with the things not to take are wallets, keys, credit cards, money and about anything else of value, because it has all, on one trip or another, gone to the bottom of the river never to be seen again. We carried our driver's licenses for identification zipped into a pocket in case our drowning body washes up somewhere unknown. We leave a car at either end of the trip, so we have transportation when we are through with our adventure. Up until now this has been a working plan.

This time after five good days on the river with no phones, no fax, no cell phone, no routine, and no anxiety other than will we live through the next drop, we came off the river in the middle of the night, found our car where we had left it, packed up and started up the road from the river heading home, telling ourselves what a really good trip this one had been.

It was a dirt, one-lane road completely grown over in some places in the middle of the dark. About a half mile up the road the car stopped. It just stopped. No noise, no leaks; it was just not running. My husband said, " Let's wait; it'll start soon, because I have a conference call at 9:00 in the morning." As if the car would consider the necessity of a conference call and start right up. I shared with him the opinion of both the car and myself on that logic and started walking up the road. Eventually I came to a road where I could see a yard light shining in the distance. Completely forgetting that I looked like a woman who had been on the river for five days, I started toward it. Of course, as I got closer, the dogs started barking, and the house lights came on, and then the porch light came on, and then a woman about my age came out. A faded quilt made an bulky cloak around her shoulders against the cold. She propped something against the inside of the door that I had no doubt was a shotgun. The sour, yeasty smell of stale beer poured over me from the open door, and she had the appearance of someone that, as my Aunt Martha would say, "drank a little." I told her what was wrong and that I had no phone, wallet or AAA card with me, but that I really was who I said I was and would do her no harm.

    She said she'd get her man up. It was now close to 3:00 A.M. He came out into the yard and said to me, "The first thing is to get that car out of the middle of the road." He kept on talking to me like we knew each other until I started to think maybe I looked like someone he really did know. He went on to say that Bill probably would be up soon, just like I had always known Bill, and that if he knew we needed him, he'd get on up here. But we needed to go into Hot Springs to get him at his filling station, because he didn't answer the phone this early, just thinking that it was a wrong number calling. So I got into his truck with him, and we rode together in the middle of the night to Hot Springs. Sure enough Bill was just having his coffee and said he'd follow us in his tow truck to where our car was stalled in the middle of the road. I decided not to tell him then that I had no credit cards, checks or wallet with me. I also decided that I wouldn't tell him I had no idea where my car was let alone where I was. But the two of them had it under control, there being only so many roads from the river that went by the house of the woman with the quilt and the gun and the nice man who got up in the middle of the night to help a stranger.

    Bill couldn't get the car started, so he towed it back to his garage, where he told us he would have to order a part to get it to start up again. The part would take several days to materialize, and in the real world the 9:00 o'clock conference call loomed again. I asked them if they knew anyone who could get us back to where we lived. The answer was no, but they said they would call around. I decided I had to tell them I had no money, but if they could get me back to my bank in my hometown, I would then be able to pay them. Now I have to tell you that after five days on the river, we looked about as bad as we could get, and the car was a twelve-year-old Buick worth about $50.00. This did not seem to bother them. I should add here that we probably looked as good as they did, but that's not saying much either.

They discussed several people who could possibly help us and settled on a man they knew who raised sheep and who was possibly up by now and might be able to help us that morning. A call was made to him, and he said he'd charge me 25 cents a mile to take us home. I would have paid him much more. So I sat in the back with the straw for the sheep on the ride home. Many prize-winning sheep had undoubtedly ridden in that station wagon, probably in the very seat where I sat. I believed what he said about raising sheep; his whole car smelled like sheep. I could have sat in the front, but he was a tobacco chewer, and he spit it into a cup fixed to the dashboard. I felt that I looked just about as bad as I was going to already, so just in case he missed his cup I chose to sit in the back on the sheep-seat. The dashboard already had some very suspicious colors on it. Since I had gotten us this far while my husband chose to sit in the car and sulk, I decided he could have the honor of riding in the front seat with our good Samaritan who chewed tobacco and spit it at the dashboard. I suppose the sheep don't mind the spitting.

Eventually we arrived safely home and things returned to normal after our adventure out into the real world. These kind people took care of us out of the goodness of their hearts, because we didn't look like we had ever had a dollar in the bank, let alone have anything of any value an hour away with which to repay them. It's good to know that there are still people like that around, especially here in our mountains. A week later they all received early Christmas presents, which I hope eased the fact that they were rudely awakened by a couple of straggly, waterlogged strangers in the middle of the night who needed their help.

ARRABELLE OHARA

Arrabelle always sat in the same rocking chair, in the same spot, surrounded by her things, wearing black or dark-blue dresses that shined in spots when the light hit them. A birdcage with a canary in it, which to her was a bidget, was always beside her. It was a messy canary. There was always a layer of seed hulls on the floor underneath the cage that was seldom swept up and often tracked all over.

She kept her things in two big old steamer trunks with round tops. She said they had round tops so that the steamship people would always keep her clothes right side up, while she was traveling on tour. She used to be young and beautiful with a contralto voice that kept her regularly employed on the European Opera circuit in the 40's and 50's. She now had white hair that stood out in different directions, and her skin was thin and white and papery because she never went outside. Her hands were now all bony with blue veins, and her eyes were filmy and gray.

She had really beautiful clothes that she never wore anymore. Maybe they were a little out of date. Sometimes I tried on her clothes that were still beautiful and new-looking even after forty years. She had an ice-green silk taffeta dress that if she would let me I would wear the rest of my life. She always wore her lace net gloves, which had the fingers cut out back to the knuckles. She owned eight pairs of these, because she needed her knuckles free for her continuing games of solitaire.

Pictures of horses, an old family picture of about 30 people and a postcard from Ireland with black-faced sheep on a hill were on the walls. A big old 1948 calendar hung in the hall noting her political affiliation. Her rooms were cold, the kind of cold no furnace could warm--the kind of cold that hadn't had any human warmth for a long time.

Sometimes she let me be fascinated with her room and wander around in it picking things up and looking at them, and sometimes she'd scream at me to sit down and be still. She had on her fireplace mantle a collection of flags. They were in various configurations, which were the representations of the ethnic backgrounds of her six husbands. I always felt that the European Opera circuit must have been just wonderfully exciting.

She was the only person who gave me such an awful sadness. I think the sadness was always right below her surface and that her surface was easily scratched, but by now I was not wholly unprepared for it. She once was quoted as saying that "bitchiness was one of her more valuable traits." It was printed in the Paris newspaper Le Monde.

She had decorated with candle stubs stuck into empty wine bottles with melted wax built up around the bottlenecks. Mice, cobwebs, darkness abounded everywhere and everything creaked. The tall weeds outside the window looked wet even in the sunshine. It wasn't a place anyone with sanity would care to visit, let alone live. I asked her once why she stayed there, and she replied, "If God doesn't favor the rich, how come they're not the poor ones?" I think this meant that her money was all gone.

She listened to me talk and said "mmmmm" like it had 15 syllables in it. Words stuck in her mouth like a burr. She had all these exciting past lives she could think about and go to them in her mind whenever she wanted to. Age was shrinking her down. Maybe instead of dying she would just disappear like milk pod puffs. Old women like her all looked strangely alike. As if age was another country they all moved to as they aged, a country of home folks with relations there that looked just like them.

There was a large wooden pier behind her house, and she liked to sit out there at night and read. She had a chair and a lamp with a really, really long extension cord. She sat out there reading and drinking cocktails. It was the only light for miles around and shone across the water. She drank her vodka out there on the pier in a bucket, which she lowered into the water with a rope to keep it cool. She drank bull shots, which I later found out were bullion and vodka. It made sense, because she always said her drink was good for her.

She's been dead for years now, but when I think of her, I like to think of her sitting in her chair under her light on the end of the pier reading something that pleased her or thinking her private thoughts of her glamorous life.

SARA PACHER, a small-town Georgia native, spent her adult life in Manhattan, Europe, San Francisco and Mexico before putting down roots in these ancient, garden-like mountains, where her ancestors had settled in 1790. She helped create both *Atlanta* and *BackHome* magazines, was an assistant editor at Prentice-Hall, Inc. and at *Western Skier* magazine, a travel editor for *Better Homes and Gardens* and a senior editor/tour director for *The Mother Earth News* magazine. Her assignments have taken her all over this country and world, and her articles have appeared in *Greenprints, Smoky Mountain Living* and *The Utne Reader*. Sara's interview with President and Mrs. Carter is reprinted in *The Engaging Reader*, a college textbook on writing. She's contributed to Rodale's gardening books and co-wrote five editions of *An Insider's Guide to the North Carolina Mountains*. Her novel of first-century Rome, *The Gladiator Isarna*, is available online and from bookstores.

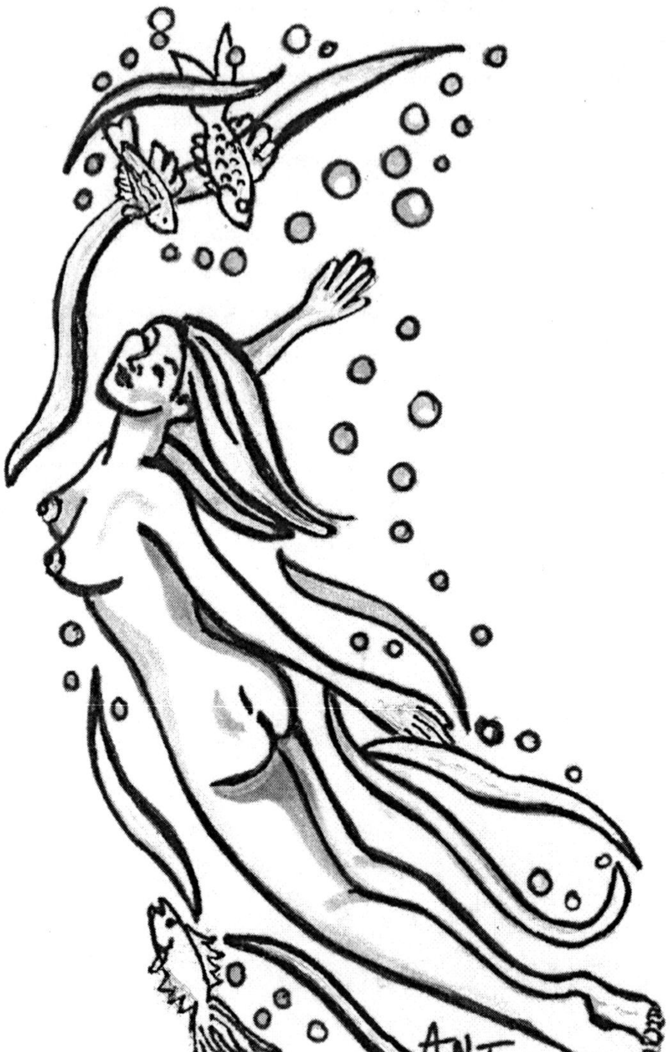
A.N.T.

GENTLY DOWN THE STREAM

Swimming, shining,
Looking for a magical sign.
Faces changing.
Loving the changes that we find.
Coming to know all things existing.
Learning to see.
Feeling it flow and not resisting.
Letting it be.
Flowing where the river goes.
Moving with the summer breeze.
Passing swiftly through the light.
Rushing down into the seas.
Here we go!
Here we go!
Let it flow!
Let it flow!

I'LL WRITE OF SIMPLE THINGS

I'll write of simple things,
like crowds and noise, hot air,
and dirty children's faces.
Rivers rolling in refuse,
and it in them.
Night which blackens fields
but leaves the cities
bright with lights.
Corn with silken tassels.
Corn with butter spread.
Teeth and greasy fingers.
A kitten's purr.
The broken sidewalk
that causes me to trip.

The feel of an oyster as it
slips down my throat
like okra
or an egg.
Simple things,
then I shall not write of you.

DECADES

One year old, and it's all so fine.
The world, I'm sure, is mine, all mine.
And if it's weird, or if it's strange,
I can always make it change
with a smile.

Ten years old, and it's getting tough.
The world out there is getting rough.
And everything I do is wrong,
But I'm learning fast, and I'm growing strong
with a smile.

Twenty years of playing at life,
Then I have a kid, and I have a wife,
And I've got two cars and a hungry dog.
Can't amble now; have to learn to jog
with a smile.

Thirty years and who am I
Still reaching for that pie in the sky?
I've learned a lot, but I haven't learned
You never get the prize you've earned
with a smile.

Forty years, and it's still all right.
I'm not about to stop the fight,
But since there's no real objection

I'd better try another direction
with a smile.

Fifty years, and I start to swear
'Cause I've come so far
But I don't know where.
Yet my friends began to join me there
with a smile.

Sixty years on down the road,
It's time to stop and lighten the load.
But who's that pretty girl passing by?
I think I might make one more try
with a smile.

Seventy years, I'm still the same,
But nobody lets me play the game.
Gotta make room for the other guy,
So I put away my suit and tie
with a smile.

Eighty years. I could tell 'em a lot,
But no one wants the wisdom I've got,
And I feel a little bit in the way,
Though they pat my back, and they say "good day"
with a smile.

Ninety years, and it's going fast.
The future has become the past.
A month is just a day or so.
I sit and watch the roses grow
with a smile.

One hundred years, and what do I win?
A pretty nurse to shave my chin
And a great big cake and an interview,
But all I've got to leave with you

is a smile,
just a smile--
remember to smile.

XANADU

Coleridge lay upon his bed,
Opium visions in his head,
When suddenly he saw a place
Alight with beauty, love and grace.
A place so fair, so far away,
It's hard to find that place today.
He called it Xanadu.

One day I was amazed to see
An angel right in front of me.
I said, "Please tell me, if you can,
Why you're an angel; I'm a man."
He laughed and said, "If you could see,
You'd know you are the same as me.
We're both Xanadu."

I said, "Your lips would not speak lies.
There's too much wisdom in your eyes.
But mine are blind; they cannot see,
And this is just a word to me."
He nodded, and he laughed again.
"Then please allow me to explain
This word Xanadu.

"'X' means God and so does 'du',
And 'du' can also stand for you.
Amuses is what 'ana' means,
Which means all this is just a dream.
Xanadu. Xanadu.

The meaning is inside of you."

Now times go by. I watch them roll
The myriad shows as they unfold:
The starlit night, the stormy day,
Knowing it's just God at play.
And I'm so glad I came to see
It's God amusing self and me.
It's all Xanadu.

Xanadu. Xanadu.
The meaning is inside of you.

ANGKOR WAT

Flying down an empty skyway,
Walking down an ancient highway,
Searching for the ruins of Eden,
Lost among the heathen.

Saffron colors, young girls singing.
Jungle temple bells are ringing.
Empty seashells full of sighing:
"All that lives is dying."

Are we loving then so vainly?
Fallen statues smile so strangely.
Astral colors forming flowers;
Rain in falling, silver showers.

Patterns carved in seas of stoneness
Tell the tale of man's aloneness.
Yet I lie beneath a tree
Feeling one with all I see.

Bird calls. Night falls.

A MIRROR POEM

Life comes to my side
And washes like a wave
Its sorrow, sin and sadness
Over the shells of my consciousness,
Which are worn—oh, so slowly—
To the form of existing time.

And soft as down, the sublime
And the good, like the lowly,
Reach my door, and I confess
I do not know which to bless.
But, no doubt, in the grave
Neither will abide.

SOME "SOMETIMES I THINK" POEMS

Sometimes I think
That I shouldn't,
But I do, or I wouldn't.
So should you.

Sometimes I think
I'm on the brink
Of thanking the rank
Who sometimes think.

Sometimes I think
That I must cry
When I look in the mirror
And see it is I.

Sometimes I think

Love is the thing
That brings spring.

Sometimes I think
That love's the cart
That to the hangman
Takes the heart.

Sometime I think,
And think,
And think.

Sometimes I think
I'd best not tell you
What I think
Sometimes.

TO AN ARTIST IN FRONT OF ST. PATRICK'S

There he is again.
I've seen him there before
Though it is winter now
And summer then
And he has grown
A little thin.

HAVE YOU?

Have you ever longed for something
That you know is out of reach
And kept that longing secret?
It was much too deep for speech.

Have you ever loved a kitten
Or a baby, or a man
And that love was much too deeply felt
For you to understand?

Have you ever walked in rain at night
And thought, "It matters not who's right?"
If so don't ask for more than now,
For more of God or why or how.

ATTITUDE

Young and wise and pretty woman
Won't you stop and tell me why
I'm too sad to go on living;
I'm too mad to think I want to die.

I keep thinking that I'm doing
All the things I know I should,
But life's dark and getting deeper,
Dark and deeper in the woods.

Tell me why my dreams are nightmares,
Why my days are full of pain.
When I'm wet there is no sunshine.
When I'm dry there is no rain.

She just laughed and reached out to me,

Laid her hand upon my head.
In a voice both sweet and gentle
This is what that wise one said:

"You were never born to suffer.
You were only born to find
Everything you see around you
Is a mirror of your mind."

THE HAIR

She was at the sink brushing her teeth when she saw a taut-wound spring of hair, coiled darkly, halfway down the white basin.

"Phifft!" she said, flashing on the various hairs she had on occasions plucked from her tongue. She aimed a little foaming spit at it and missed. She spit again, and this time the foam avalanched down the sink, caught the hair and slid with it slowly, slowly, slowly toward the round, dark drain hole. As the hair slithered along, struggling against the enveloping, foamy mass, she became caught up in its mystery and began to study it.

Obviously, it wasn't off her body. It was too dark. It was very like one of the sparse, cute hairs that looped around Jean-Paul's dark, sensitive nipples. Who knows? Perhaps that very hair had rested over his sweet, young heart. But, no. It was too fine and curly. Probably the hair wasn't from his broad, hard chest at all. Probably it was ....

She hadn't even finished the thought before a surge of desire simultaneously rushed up through her belly to her heart and down to her toes, making her legs weak. He lay just a few feet away. Without even looking she knew every detail of his beautiful, sensuous body. He was sleeping on his stomach, one arm shading his exquisitely sculptured face from the afternoon sun and the other stretched out across the bed, still enveloping the spot where she had been.

Just then the foam reached the drain and--gullup!--down it

went. But, miraculously, the suddenly sacred hair was left clinging with all its might to the metal rim.

Quickly, she reached down to pull the precious, little darling to safety. At the same time, the hair seemed to leap up to her hand. It was so sudden and unexpected that she jumped back from the sink only to find it clutching her index finger.

She shook it violently, but it kept its wire-tight grip. She rubbed it on the edge of the sink. It was still there! She panicked. Without thinking she turned on the cold water, and–whoosh!–it was gone. Down the drain!

For a moment she stood in complete shock at her cruel and heartless act. Leaning against the sink she watched the water swirling away as predictably as time and began to realize that sentimental attachment was a nuisance that she really didn't need and probably wouldn't miss a bit.

She rinsed her mouth and toothbrush and quietly packed her bag. She left a heartfelt note that read: "Jean-Paul, I'll always love you. Lisa."

The train to Barcelona was right on time.

BETTY J. REED is a native and life-long resident of Western North Carolina. She is the author of *The Brevard Rosenwald School* published by McFarland in 2004, for which she received a certificate of commendation from The American Association for State and Local History. Currently she is an instructor at The Transylvania Center of Blue Ridge Community College. Her interests include Appalachian history, educational history and creative writing.

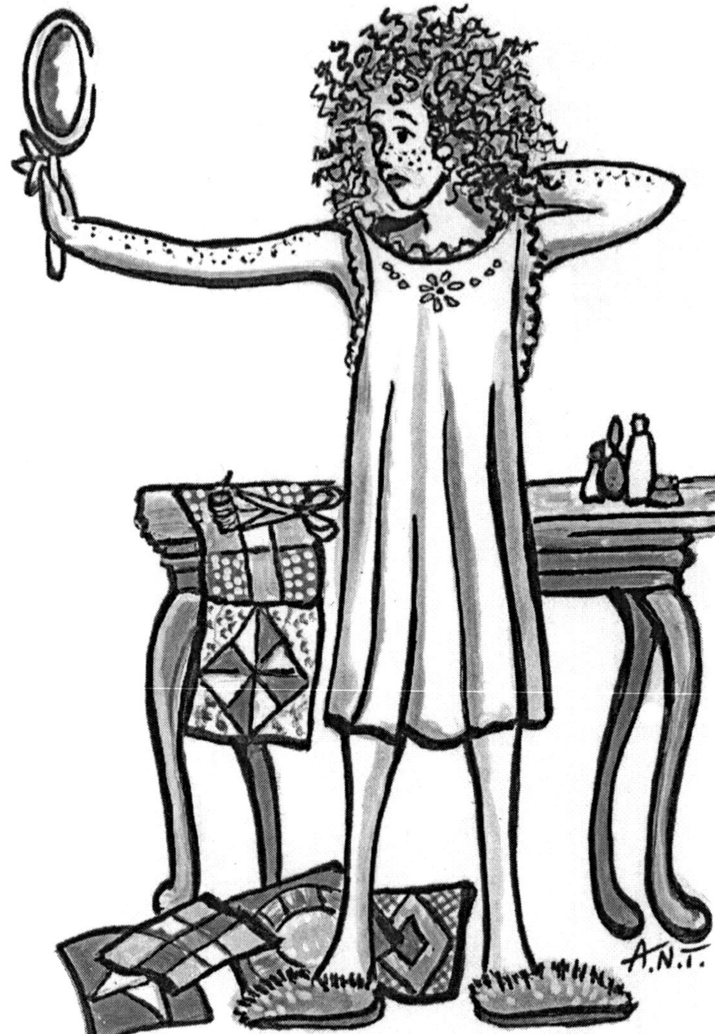
A.N.T.

A DAZZLING AUTUMN AT THE PINK BEDS
Dedicated to Caleb Sizemore

Nellie studied her reflection in a hand-held mirror and felt unhappy looking at herself. "Why can't I look like everyone else?" she wondered aloud.

"What's this I hear? Put that mirror down and get in here. We're going to have ourselves a little talk," called Granny, who sat in her rocker facing Nellie's door.

As she pushed her coppery hair away from her face, Nellie took a final glance at the freckled, button-nosed face in the mirror and complained, "I'm just plain ugly." But she walked into the living room as quickly as her eleven-year-old legs would allow, stretched out on the hooked rug at Granny's feet and met the sixty-one-year-old's glance straight on.

"Child, how you look is just fine. God made you, and He don't make mistakes. Hand me that basket of scraps for my quilting, and listen to me while I piece a square." Nellie knew that Granny believed idle hands were the devil's workshop and wasn't surprised to hear her add, "You know, you could piece one while we talk, if you like. Just don't make your stitches too long; keep 'em neat and tight." Granny placed the colorful scraps across her lap and proceeded to lick the end of the thread and loop it through the eye of the needle. "If we all looked too much alike, we'd be the dullest crowd on the planet. Think about your friends. They sure don't look like one another. And, I bet you wouldn't want them to. Now your hair may be unruly in this weather, but a good haircut can help with that. Monotony, is that what you want? The very idea! Looking like everyone else. All blondes, all brunettes, all redheads! Boring! The same ole same ole! How interesting is that?" As Nellie propped up against the hassock, she eyed the pile of quilting scraps, picking out the bright greens and oranges, reds and yellows in designs of blocks and stripes, and spread them on the floor in a near-star pattern. She pulled an already-threaded needle from the pin cushion, and pulling her coppery brows together knotted the thread, and began slowly and carefully to sew two pieces together.

"I just don't like how I look. I hate my freckles and my hair looks wild. Everybody else has smooth skin, all one color; why, even my eyes are speckled."

"Your eyes are a lovely hazel, just like your father's. Now, enough complainin.' Let me tell you a story. It might help you appreciate your looks." Granny was an instant story-maker and Nellie relaxed as she wondered what this new tale would be about. "Now, let's see," continued Granny, as a plot began taking shape. "There was a family of trees living near the Pink Beds in Pisgah National Forest, and it was mid-summer. The grown-up trees were feeling sad because in the past lots of folks came there to picnic and to enjoy the out-of doors, but their neighborhood was no longer a popular stop for human families."

'Nowadays,' said one, 'folks like to motorcycle to the top of the mountain and ride on the Parkway or follow the Davidson River trails on horseback. No one lingers here anymore, and I miss the good old days when folks had a happy time in our shade.'

"While the adults were missing times past, would you believe it? The tree children were voicing just the opposite of what you said, Nellie. Their tale of woe was, 'We are all alike. Why can't we be some color other than green? It's no fun being like everyone else.' Well, here is what happened."

"All the young saplings, maple and poplar and birch, were remarkably alike in the spring and summer that year. Although their leaves ranged from hunter to lime green, forest green could get mighty monotonous. One proud young fellow, Arby, invited all the trees to admire his blue-green foliage. 'Look close, and you can see I am not just green; I have some sky color mixed in. It's beautiful, but you have to look really close, or I'll seem totally green.'

His generous-hearted younger sister, Lita, admitted that if she gave his foliage a really close look she could see a trace of blue, but it took a lot of squinting. 'But, Lita, I see some pretty yellow highlights mixed in with your green,' assured Lance, another youngster in the grove. 'You're not totally green either.'

Then their chatter was interrupted by the booming voice of Great-Poppa Oak, 'In the fall changes will come. You little scrawny saplings will see reds and oranges and yellows, and yes, every hue of brown, color those beautiful green leaves. Now, that will give you something to talk about.' Excited by Great-Poppa's predictions, the little trees began bragging about the colors they would be. Their thoughts tumbled out in torrents.

'Promise we won't all be the same. We won't have to search to find our differences. Really? We'll each be truly different.' The possibilities seemed endless.

'Oh, I want to be totally red. Can I be? Can I?' begged Arby.

'No, no, I want to be red,' insisted Lita.

'Let's all be different,' said Lance. 'Can we, Great-Poppa? Can we make our own patterns?'

'Well, yes, if you'll stop this arguing. I need a little peace in our grove. I'm not as young as I used to be. Just settle down. Yes, I can let you create your own designs. It will take a lot of energy, but it can be done. Just be sure you'll be happy with the result, for you must keep your design until winter comes.'

'How can I keep Arby and Lita from stealing my color plan? I don't want them copying my ideas,' said Lance.

'Well, let's see. I need to think,' boomed Great-Poppa. 'You can send messages by your special pal, Winnie the Breeze. Whenever he's awake and in the neighborhood, just whisper your plan to him and he will whisper it to me. And Mother Nature and I will make arrangements. But, I must warn you again. Give it a lot of thought. Make sure you'll be happy with your color scheme.'

"With Winnie's help, each of the youngsters shared his ideas secretly with Great-Poppa Oak, but as the time drew near for the fall coloring, the threesome made frequent changes for each wanted to outdo the other. By nature they were competitive. 'When will fall be here? How much longer do we have to wait? We're tired of looking so much alike.' The inquisitive youngsters were full of impatient questions."

'Our fall starts near the end of September, but it will take a few days before your colors are definite. And Jack Frost will add his own special touches. I can't do anything about that, but the overall design will be the one you asked for,' assured Great-Poppa. 'Try to be patient. The time for change will soon be here.'

"Finally, September 21 rolled around. At first there were

only hints of the patterns the colors would make, but with the cool breath of Jack Frost, the colors solidified into a panorama of bright and dazzling and muted and dull hues. Not being able to see themselves fully was a bit frustrating for the young trees, but for a change the competitive threesome praised one another and received compliments in return."

'You are so beautiful! How did you dream up such a splendid design?' "No hint of animosity or jealousy underscored their admiring comments."

"One family of humans stopped by to picnic and looked in open-mouthed astonishment at the beauty in that small grove. Soon their relatives were traveling to the Pink Beds to check out reports of unusual fall colors. Word spread rapidly. The rangers thought their newsletter should carry an article about the unique color patterns. Soon rangers from other sites took the time to drop by and enjoy the view. And motorcyclists heard about the extraordinary colors and took a side trip to feast their eyes on the gorgeous trees. Horseback riders veered from the trail and looked appreciatively at Lita, Arby, and Lance, who basked unashamedly in their admiration. All this man-given attention made the grown-up trees happy because once again human families were lounging in their shade. It was a joyful autumn. However, one cool morning, snow flurried through the Pink Beds. Each tree, old and young alike, had flakes of white drifting in and lodging on their colored leaves. The result was spectacular."

"Great-Poppa Oak reminded the youngsters that their leaves would begin to fall and that a winter nap would follow. 'But when you wake up in the spring, you will be sprouting green leaves again. Do you think you can appreciate that color when the time comes?' "

"Yawning already, the saplings welcomed the coming of a new growth of green leaves, but each was happy that for a season there had been a chance to be truly different. And the entire tree community basked in delight that picnickers and hikers had once again flocked to their neighborhood."

Nellie handed her quilting piece to her grandmother saying, "Granny, that was a good story. Here, I've finished my star for your quilt. Mine's a lot different from yours. I hope my stitches are close enough. Thanks for telling me a story. And, even if I don't like my looks, I'm glad that you do."

Granny reached down and gave her a hug. She knew that her granddaughter would become even more beautiful in time.

SPECIAL NOTE:

In the southwestern section of North Carolina is the beautiful Pisgah National Forest. It was established from lands once belonging to George W. Vanderbilt, who hired Dr. Carl Schenck to bring the technology of the Industrial Revolution to the forest. The Cradle of Forestry is located there and preserves the history of forestry. Lessons are taught about the importance of conservation with puppets, puzzles, costumes, movies, and hikes. The Cradle of Forestry also describes life in the Appalachian region during the 20th century. Mountaineers had to use the materials provided by the forest in order to survive. Those were nature's gifts to the settlers. Woodsmen, blacksmiths, quilters, and spinners demonstrate their skills on the Biltmore Campus Trail. An old sawmill may be visited. Not far away in a high mountain valley is an area called the Pink Beds. In the spring, mountain laurel, wild azaleas, and rhododendron bloom there, and that is how the name came to be "Pink Beds."

SISTER'S DILEMMA

"I never thought I would call you an angel, but I just did," I told my younger sister. I had been exploring Oprah Winfrey's website and discovered her practice of honoring some folks who were "angels" in their communities. Because my sister is a foster parent who has mentored over one hundred children, I impulsively decided she would be a good candidate and proceeded to fill out the nomination form, and the positive effect it had on Peggy convinced me I had done the right thing. When her supervisors learned that I had submitted her name to the Oprah Angel Network, they also endorsed her as an "angel."

From a sibling perspective this angel business was getting out of hand. Peggy overheard one first grader whispering in awed tones: "She's an angel" and her status as a nominated "angel" was emblazoned on the school's billboard. Remembering childhood fights in which we pulled hair and scratched, I doubted my endorsement was appropriate. I remembered on one occasion when during a physical confrontation, we froze in pretzel-like form as our mother peeped into the living room to investigate. "Oh," said Mother, "I thought something was going on." That comment reduced us to giggles, and we promptly forgot our argument. Once we fought under a towering oak in our front yard for the privilege of being the first to open a package from our sailor brother only to discover it contained his old clothes sent home for safekeeping. But excited by the "angel" nomination, Peggy's voice had a lilt to it each time we spoke. Perhaps I had done the right thing. Peggy has had an amazing influence on the children she has served. Mother's Day can be very exciting at her house. She may receive a telephone call from a serviceman stationed in Japan, or she may hear from a young man incarcerated in prison. Many call her "mother."

Peggy and I grew up in a small community in Western North Carolina, barefoot girls in an Appalachian community. We shared baths in a galvanized steel tub and felt quite elegant when our parents bought a let-down couch that became our bed. I remember how proud I was when my baby sister was chosen to be "Sunshine," the starring role in her first class play and how angry she became when I went to battle against boys who were teasing her on the playground. I had to stand up for my baby sister, but she wanted no part of it. She made it clear that she would fight her own battles. On social occasions often when our eyes met, it was telepathic that each knew wordlessly what the other was thinking at that moment.

As the years passed, we stood up for one another. Growing up in an alcoholic home created some real problems. In the midst of violent scenes we would leave home in the middle of the night, sometimes seeking refuge with relatives and sometimes sleeping in our car. At home if heavy drinking took place, we would close the blinds and keep the door shut to discourage visitors.

We found solace in church and in school, because in those places there was reprieve from turmoil, and we became prayer partners. As teenagers we claimed the promise of Scripture that if any two agree as touching any one thing, it shall be done. And often our prayers were answered in a very tangible way. When our life experiences led us in different directions, any unheralded event led to a phone call asking for sisterly support or sharing a funny or rewarding experience.

In these years that claim us among the ranks of senior citizens we have the habit of calling one another whenever any acquaintance is in need of prayer. My sister may say, "Evelyn is having tests. Please pray for the Lord's intervention." Or "Our friend is so depressed. She has had five deaths in her immediate family within six months, and she is suffering."

At other times we shared concerns about our children. Upon hearing from her, I would begin a prayer vigil, knowing that when I needed someone to count on, my sister was only a phone call away.

An unwanted call came in late spring of 2004. My sister had experienced a mild heart attack. Her doctor predicted a safe future if she followed his directions, but a week or so later she had terrific pain in her stomach and diaphragm. Diagnosed with a kidney infection, she took the prescribed medication and experienced some relief, but the pain persisted. The doctor looked for other answers.

When I called her home on the day she was to learn the results of extensive testing, one of her foster sons answered the telephone, but seemed unwilling to let me speak to her. When I persisted, he said, "Mom hasn't come inside yet. She's still in the car." Something about his young voice filled me with apprehension. An hour later I called my sister's daughter, "Mama doesn't want to talk to you," she said. "The news was not good, and she is on a crying jag." The next morning a calm Peggy shared her prognosis with me. With no hint of self-pity, she told me she had cancer of both the stomach and the liver. Her doctor described it as inoperable and incurable.

Matter-of-factly she said, "Well, I have cancer," and went on to describe a program of treatment intended to arrest its growth. "And I love my doctor." She continued. "He is a Korean American, and he is a Christian. Practically the first thing he asked me was, 'Do you have a faith?'"

Then she told me that she believed God had a purpose in allowing her to suffer and described her adopted son's response. A sweet young man, Josh is autistic and has difficulty expressing himself. Upon seeing his mother walk to a nearby house, he had followed suit but stood outside the gate. He remained there, looking a bit lost until Eddie, his father, called him inside. Only then did he walk through the gate. He entered the house and wordlessly kissed his mother and then walked back home. When his parents returned home, Josh shared this wish with his father, "I told Jesus to let me hurt instead of her." Peggy was deeply touched when she learned of Josh's concern. He would have preferred to be the cancer's victim.

Her ordeal reflects that of other cancer patients and their families. At times we are distraught and depressed. She has been confronted with fatigue and its fragmenting effect on her physical stamina. At times we struggle to understand how and why and hope for a break-through. The battles are endless--against disease, against pain, against insurance regulations, against pity, against bureaucracy, against the odds.

Her campaigns focus on denying the inevitable by persisting in church attendance, by overcoming her sense of weakness, and most of all by focusing on hope. She is determined to live by dealing with each day's challenges. Two weeks during the summer of 2004, she was energized by attending Vacation Bible School at her church. I had suggested she avoid crowds, but she wanted to continue participating in church services.

I have always been jealous of her beautiful blonde hair. "I think I will just shave off what's left," she said. "It has fallen out in patches." Seeing her turbaned head, I remembered her asking me to cut her hair when she was about eight years old. "I am sick of these pigtails," she said. Well, under that same oak where we had struggled over Brother's package, I took the scissors and cut each pigtail. Crying and screaming followed. She was not happy with my efforts and swore enmity against me forever. Soon, however, that beautiful wavy blond hair was her crowning glory, and she had forgotten my failure as a barber.

If I thought, however reluctantly, that she could be called an angel before this experience, I am now convinced that she deserves that title. She reaches out to all of us who love her assuring us that God is in control and that she is His willing tool. We are sisters. There is a bond that even death, when it comes for either of us, cannot erase, but for now there is hope that this angel, my sister, will survive.

Update: *Peggy Jamerson Owen's life ended in the spring of 2005 at a time when the world was challenged by the fate of Terri Schiavo and the death of a beloved Pope.*

SISTER

"Now, don't forget I love you,"
whispered her sweet lips.
"Pray for me. I'll pray for you."
Now lying alone in her grave,
body still, agony free, but
her voice echoes
this constant plea and promise,
"Pray for me. I'll pray for you."
I had begged, "God, please,
no more suffering.
Destroy that disease."
And death, a kind of healing,
has ended her pain.

ISABELLE REINER was born in Ohio, where she worked for a time on a newspaper. She has also lived in Los Angeles, where she worked for AAA. She moved to Brevard with her husband in 1991. She has written her memoirs for her family as well as poetry for the Transylvania Writers' Alliance.

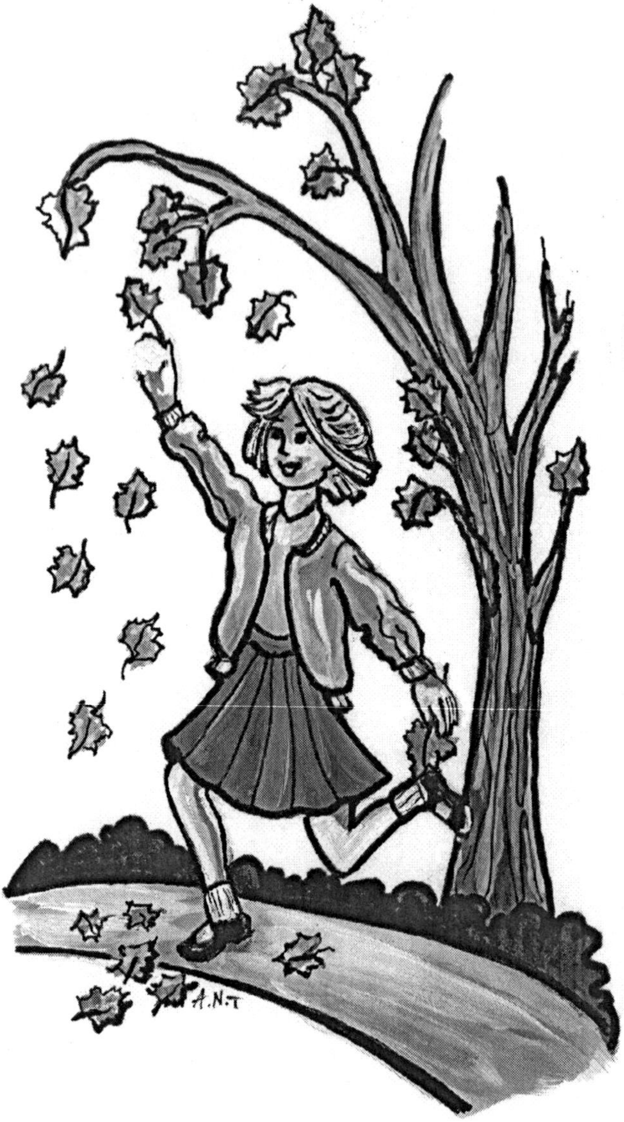
A.N.T

AS NIGHT FOLLOWS DAY—
SO DO THE SEASONS FOLLOW
EACH OTHER

Each season change is like watching a new life begin
A baby comes upon the scene "wailing" like the winds of Winter
Spring tells her—there are things to explore—
Butterflies and hummingbirds—so quick- just a blink of an eye!
Flowering trees and bushes—dressed in their colorful finery
Simply take her breath away.
Summer lets her know—she can't stay out too long—
The sun will burn and the bugs will bite.
Autumn—the air is fresh—leaf colors are brilliant, soon the leaves
    begin to fall—
She wants to chase each one as they dance their way to the
    ground—
She giggles in sheer delight.
She will grow—and change like the seasons.

DEVON SMITH has grown up in Brevard. He is a graduate of Brevard High School. He received his associate's degree in Office Systems Technology at Blue Ridge Community College in June 2004. His active imagination delights in the complex world of science fiction.

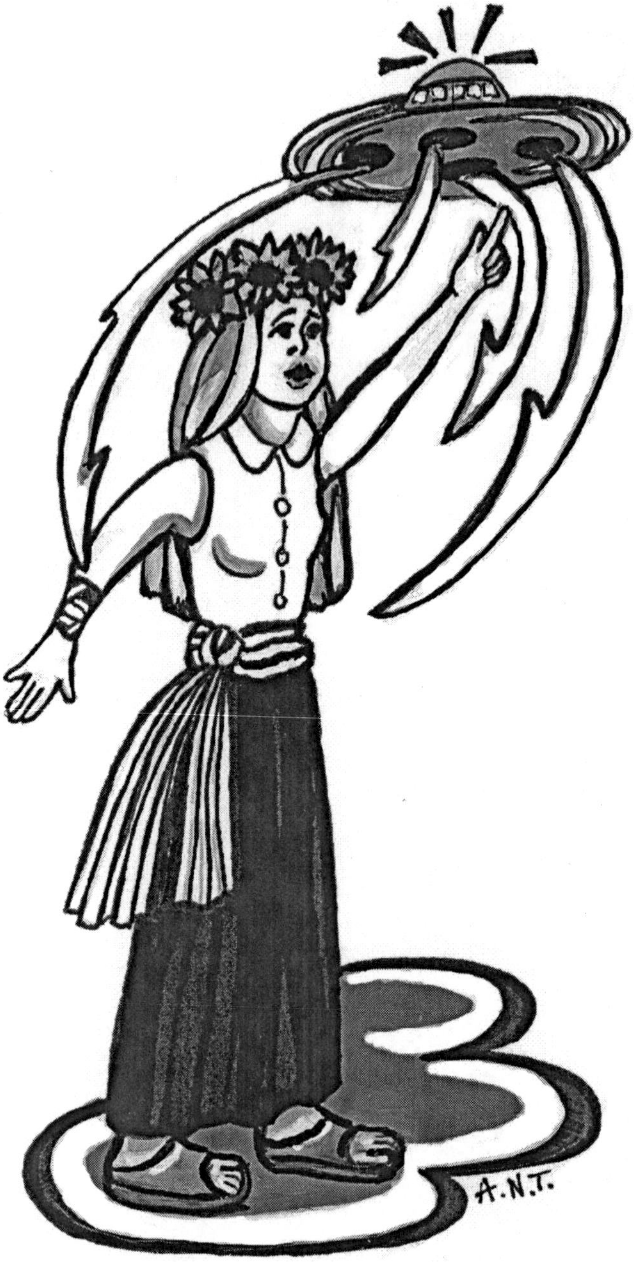
A.N.T.

THE IRON CLOUDS

The first of *The Iron Cloud Chronicles,* a work in progress

As the sun rose over one of the last villages of humanity, the people of the village began to wake. They went about their daily lives, tending their animals, preparing meals, and getting ready to work in the nearby quarry. In the distance, over the remains of an old ruined city, a large, round, saucer-shaped object hovered like a ominous black storm cloud in the sky. Often, many in the village would pause to stare at the distant saucer. Others would bow or fall to their knees and whisper to themselves before returning to their tasks.

On this day in the village, a young girl was at her window looking out at the saucer. Her red hair flowed over her shoulders and floated in the breeze. Her mother came into the room with clean clothes that had just dried on the line. As she placed the clothes on the girl's bed, her daughter turned from the window and smiled. "Thank you, Mother," she said.

"Ah, Amy," her mother sighed, "It's amazing how time flies. It seems like only yesterday that you were a babe in my arms. Now, in two days, you're going to become a prophet."

"I'm still going to be me," her daughter said, crossing the room to give her a reassuring hug and was rewarded with a smile.

"Yes, but you'll have the power to share the wisdom of the great Iron Cloud with us," she said, gesturing in the direction of the saucer. "You'll tell the people how much to dig in the quarry, when to plant our crops, and where to hunt for food."

"I won't have that much power!" Amy laughed, releasing her. "The other prophets will be there."

Later that morning, as she was helping her mother hang up more laundry, Amy asked, "Will I be the youngest prophet ever? How old were the first prophets?"

The mother thought for a moment. "Well, the first leaders were young when they were chosen. But I don't think any of them were as young as sixteen."

Pinning a sheet up to the line, Amy reminded her, "I'll be seventeen in a few months."

Just then a young man passed nearby. "Hey Amy!" he called out. She turned and waved to him. "Who is that?" her mother asked with a teasing sparkle in her eyes.

Amy smiled slightly. "No one. Just a friend."

"Is it someone whom we should invite to dinner tonight?" her mother asked.

"No, tonight's meal should just be for us. You know—just for family." Her mother dropped her eyes to the ground. "What?" Amy asked.

"Prophet Turner is coming by for dinner tonight."

Amy rolled her eyes in response. "Why? You know how I feel about him!"

"He just wants to see you before the ceremony tomorrow night. Anyway you'll have to get used to being around him when you become a prophet," her mother reminded her.

Nothing else was said as they hung the last of the laundry and went inside.

That night, when setting the table, her mother put a third place at the table. It recalled to mind those days when Amy's father was still alive and shared their meals, but a knock on the door brought her back to the present. Her mother answered it to find Turner standing in the doorway. He was a tall yet slender man. His white hair hung to his shoulders. On his head was the usual tall black buckle hat the leaders wore.

"Oh, Prophet Turner, come in. You're early." She stood aside to let him enter their home.

"Thank you for letting me come," he said politely. She nodded and bustled over to the stove. He turned to Amy. "How are you? Looking forward to tomorrow night?" he asked.

"Yes, I am," Amy said with an expressionless face.

"The fire has just gotten going, but the meal should be ready soon," Amy's mother said, stoking the fire. Turner took off his hat and hung it up as he continued to look at Amy. She stood there uncomfortably, until her mother said, "Amy, see Head Prophet Turner to his seat."

Turner raised his hand and smiled. "Please! Call me Mr. Turner. You don't have to use my title—at least not now." When he was seated, Amy joined him at the table and listened quietly as he made small talk with her mother. During the meal, Amy concentrated mostly on her food, because every time she looked up Prophet Turner was watching her. When that happened, he would smile and return to eating his own soup. Amy felt uneasy throughout the whole meal. When they had eaten, Turner asked his hostess if he could have a moment alone with Amy.

"Oh, yes, of course." As she began to clear the table, Turner got up from his chair and extended his hand to Amy. "Come, I wish to talk to you."

She ignored his hand and walked toward the door, but she didn't want to be alone with him. She stopped halfway there and turned to him. "Yes?" she questioned.

Turner smiled indulgently down at her. "Amy, I understand if you are hesitant about becoming a prophet. But you should be honored. You are the third person to become a new prophet this year. As we first prophets get older, it will be up to you younger ones to take our place. We see great potential in you to become a strong leader. Maybe someday you will take my position as head prophet." He placed a hand on Amy's shoulder. "I know you don't like me very much, ever since that incident took your father from us. But as a prophet you will come to look beyond such things and start to think and act for the good of the village." Amy's eyes blurred, and she brushed away a tear before it tumbled down her cheek. Turner removed his hand from Amy's shoulder and continued. "When I was chosen to become a prophet, I was asleep." Turner took off his black coat and revealed his white shirt. "When I woke up I found this." He rolled up the sleeve on his left arm and showed her the mark there. It was a strange, black, rectangle with slanted lines in it. "Tomorrow, you will be given a mark just like this one. This will allow you to enter the great Iron Cloud over the old city. There, they will teach you the same as the other prophets and I were taught." Amy ran her hand over Turner's mark. The black part felt smooth, but the lines within it were raised.

"Does it hurt?" she asked as she looked up at Turner.

He smiled, "You know, the last two prophets before you asked me the same thing. And I will tell you the same thing I told them. No, it doesn't hurt," he said in a reassuring voice. Turner rolled down his sleeve and put on his coat. Amy's mother came over to them and placed her arm around Amy's shoulders. Turner took his hat off the hook on the wall. "Well, I look forward to seeing you both tomorrow at the ceremony." Then he put on his hat and left .

The next night, everyone gathered in the center of the village around a large circular stone altar. At the base of the altar, separating it from the crowd, was a circle of torches illuminating the stone. In the crowd, Amy found herself surrounded by a few people dressed like Prophet Turner. He was standing near the altar in the shadow of the torch light. Amy turned to a young man a few years older than she, but still younger than the other prophets. "Marcus?" she whispered to him. Marcus leaned in. "Last night, Head Prophet Turner came by my house and showed me the mark." Marcus nodded his head. "I asked him if it was going to hurt, and he said it won't. I remember when you got the mark, but I couldn't tell if it hurt."

"Don't worry, it won't hurt." He clasped her shoulder reassuringly. Just then, Turner stood up on the altar, and the crowd went silent. Turner extended his hand to the crowd. Amy and the other prophets moved to the front of the crowd and were now facing Turner. Amy was moved to the forefront by the other prophets. She was wearing a sleeveless blouse and a long black skirt. A ring of sunflowers, a gift from her mother, crowned her head. Amy began to walk slowly up the altar's steps. She knelt before the altar, placing her arm over it. As she bowed her head, the Iron Cloud began to glow in the distance. Its light brightened up the sky. A smaller light came flying from it. The Iron Cloud went dark as the smaller light came closer to the village.

As the light approached, its bell-like shape could be seen. It flew over the crowd once, showing off its glowing underbelly. Spider-like legs began to appear it as it landed next to the altar. Amy tilted her head up slightly and saw a small opening in the front of the machine. Then two large red glowing lights appeared as though it was looking at her. She bowed her head again as a long rod-like metallic arm extended from beneath its undercarriage. At the end of the arm was a rectangular box. Now the box was over Amy's left arm. She closed her eyes as she felt it touch her skin. She was about take a deep breath, but her eyes and mouth opened wide and her breath froze as she felt a pain shoot through her arm. It lasted for a few long moments. Amy kept her head down. When the pain went away, she looked up and saw the metal arm return to the machine. It lifted off the ground, flew over the crowd once, and returned to the Iron Cloud. As the Cloud lit up once more, Turner took Amy's arm from the altar and held it high over her head for the crowd to see. The crowd began to cheer and clap. Bewildered, she saw her mother applauding with the rest. The light from the Cloud began to fade as the crowd continued to cheer.

After the ceremony, Amy was escorted to a house just outside the village. Next to it was a circle of black stones. Inside the house there was nothing but a bed and a wooden stool. She had not spoken since the ceremony. Looking down at her mark, she saw it was identical to the one on Prophet Turner's arm. But the raised lines in hers were red.

Marcus, who was standing next to her, said softly, "Don't worry. The red will be gone by tomorrow." As he touched her shoulder, Amy smiled slightly, reached up, and took his hand. They dropped their hands as Prophet Turner entered the house.

He stood unsmiling in the doorway. "Tomorrow night, you will stand in the black circle and wait for another one of the Iron Cloud's servants to take you to it. There you will become one of us. Here is where you'll stay until then." He turned and left the house.

Marcus smiled at her. "It won't be long now." She hugged him. "I'll be outside the house if you need me," he said as the other prophets left.

Amy sat quietly for hours thinking about all that had happened. She wondered why Turner and Marcus had lied to her. She remembered when her father had died in the quarry, and the Iron Cloud had done nothing to save his life. "If The Iron Cloud is so great, why didn't it save him?" she thought to herself. She got up from the stool and peered out a small window near the door. She could see Marcus leaning up against the house, arms crossed and head down, almost as if he were asleep. His buckle hat was tilted over his eyes. Quietly, Amy opened the door of the house and tried to slowly creep past Marcus. She got a few feet away before she heard his voice.

"And where are you going?" Amy turned and saw Marcus raise his head. "You know you're not supposed to leave here before tomorrow night," he said with a smile.

Amy smiled back coyly, "I–I just wanted to go see my mother one last time before tomorrow." Marcus moved towards her, but just as he was reaching for her arm, he suddenly fell to the ground with a strange dart-like object sticking from his back. Frightened, she started to scurry back to the house, but just as she reached the door, a figure stepped from the darkness and grabbed her. Amy felt a cloth cover her mouth. Then everything went dark.

As Amy's eyes opened to early morning light, she could feel the wind blowing across her face. She shook her head to clear it and began to look around. She saw trees, rocks, and the ground moving swiftly around her. She couldn't believe how fast she was going. She looked down and saw that her hands were bound. She tried to scream but couldn't. There was something over her mouth. She leaned against the side of the cart as it began to shake violently. She felt every bump and dip in the ground that went under her. Across from her, a figure hunched over holding on to a pair of handles connected to the front wheel of the vehicle. The figure was wearing a long black patchwork coat. It seemed to be made out made of leather. On his head was a black hat with a stiff rim that didn't seem to move in the wind. She felt deafened by a blaring noise like an enraged bear that was coming from a dirty rusted machine that seem to be powering the vehicle. Amy then noticed sacks and other strange things on the rear of the machine behind the figure. Next to her, she could see a long rifle-like thing strapped to the side cart. Over her legs, tied to the top of the side cart was a worn bed roll.

As her forced, uncomfortable journey continued, Amy recognized less and less of her surroundings. The vehicle finally came to a stop. The man climbed off and began to go through the sacks attached to the back. His face was hidden behind dark black goggles and scarf. He took out a round metal object from one of the sacks and began to twist a knob until it came off. Turning away from her, he pulled down the scarf from his face and raised the object as if he were drinking something out of it. He then unbuttoned his coat and pulled out something. He knelt down on the ground and examined it. Amy tried to shift into a more comfortable position and caught her bonds against the rough edge of the side cart. That gave her an idea. She began to rub her bonds up against that area. Surprisingly, they quickly came undone. She untied her legs and took off the gag. Cautiously, she got up out of the side cart and stumbled on a thick branch lying on the ground. She picked it up and slowly made her way around the vehicle without the figure seeing her. She raised the branch over her head and sneaked up behind the man, who was studying a strange-looking paper with lines and colors on it.

As he turned and looked up, Amy, with all her might, brought the branch down, hitting the man on the head and knocking off his hat. He fell to the ground hard, face first. When she saw him trying to get up, she brought the branch down again over his back. The man groaned as he turned over. When Amy raised the branch once again, he put his hands up over his face. She could see patches of white hair sticking up around his head. "Wait! Wait! I'm not your enemy!" He jerked off his goggles. The eyes that looked up at her were weary, yet friendly.

"Who--who are you?" Amy gasped. As she lowered the branch, the man lowered his hands.

He sat up and rubbed his back. "I'm--from outside of the village."

Amy raised the branch again. "That's impossible! There is nothing outside of the village."

Raising his hands again, he yelled, "Yes, there is!" Though Amy stood ready to strike again, the man seemed to relax. "Who told you that? Those machines from those ships or your leaders?"

Amy looked bewildered. "How do you...?"

"How do I know about those machines? I've been watching you in the village for quite some time now," he explained. Though still on guard, Amy lowered the branch as the man got to his feet. "I hid myself in the forests near your village. I saw everything: your taking that mark on your arm, being taken to that house. Everything." The man turned back to his vehicle. "I wore that to conceal myself." He pointed towards a strange looking suit lying over the sack on the back of the vehicle. "There is a technical name for it, but I call it my watcher's suit," he said with a smile.

Recalling what happened during the night, Amy was far from sure that she could trust him. "What did you do to Marcus and me?" she demanded. "What was that thing that was sticking out of his back?"

"It was just a simple tranquilizer. Marcus will be fine now. I used something similar on you, and you're okay now, aren't you? Just put down the stick."

Amy clinched the branch tighter. "Why?"

Realizing that Amy wasn't going to give up the branch, he shrugged and turned his attention to his vehicle, giving Amy her chance to flee. "You won't find your way. You'll be lost forever," the man called. She stopped and faced him, still clutching the branch.

"Why?" Amy asked again.

"We're at least twenty miles from your village." Amy looked bewildered. "We're very far away. Even if you knew where to go, it would be well after nightfall before you got back there." The man slowly approached. "Tell me, how do you think the city near your village came to be in ruins? What have they told you?"

Amy began to back away from him. "Why? Don't you know?"

"No. I don't," the man said as he paused.

"When I was young, I was taught that after mankind had destroyed itself—after a great war—the Iron Clouds...."

"The Iron what?" the man interrupted.

"It's what we call the things in the sky," Amy said.

"Oh, those things. I see. Continue."

"After the war, the Iron Clouds came down and saved many of our people like my parents. They placed them in villages all over the world. Ever since then, the Clouds, through our prophets, have guided our people. They show us how to hunt, how to farm, and in exchange we helped them mine the quarry."

"I see," said the man. "Who are these prophets?"

"After the Iron Clouds brought our people to the villages,

several awoke with marks like these on their bodies," Amy said as she pointed to the mark was on her arm. "They then began to tell the others about what happened. They were chosen by the Clouds to be our leaders--the prophets of the Iron Clouds."

"Where did those things get that name. Why did you start calling them that?" Amy tried to remember. "There was a woman in our village who was blind. She asked the head prophet what the things in the sky looked like. He told her how they floated like clouds in the sky, but they were made out of a metal like iron. She said, 'So they are like Iron Clouds.' The prophets began to refer to them as the Iron Clouds."

"I see," the man said as he turned away from Amy. "What if I told you that all those things you were told about the Clouds are lies?"

Amy's eyes widened. "What do you mean?"

The man turned back to Amy. "What if I were to tell you it was the Clouds that caused the destruction, not a war?" Amy shook her head in disbelief as he continued. "That they rounded up your parents and others like them and put them in those villages."

"Then why didn't...?" Amy started to ask, but the man interrupted. "Because the clouds must have erased their memories of what really happened." He reached into his coat and pulled out a small rectangular item with a screen on it. Under the screen were a few buttons. The man pressed a large button on the device and the screen lit up. Amy watched as the man touched the screen. After a few moments the man turned the device around and showed it to her. She stood in shock as an image appeared on the screen. She had never seen such a thing. A woman was standing in a strange place; on a wide strip of earth that was black with white lines running down the center and along the sides. She pointed up, as the picture then turned up to show that something was approaching the woman. Amy stood breathless as she realized what the object was. It was an Iron Cloud. The woman tried to talk but there was no sound. Then beams shot out from the Cloud. Several structures in the distance began to topple as dust and smoke came flying through the air. The image moved around wildly, then focused on the woman again.

Amy looked at the woman more closely. She realized who the woman was.

Her mouth moved slowly, as she cried, "Mother?" and reached for the device.

"That was one of the last scenes those of us who fled ever saw of her. After that, the city was left in ruins," the old man said softly. Tears began to run down Amy's face. The branch that she once held so tightly fell to the ground. Amy followed it, falling to her knees and burying her face in her arms. The man placed the device back into his coat. He placed a gentle arm around her shoulders and tried to comfort her.

An hour after the man had shown the images to Amy, she sat just a few feet away from the vehicle while the man continued to look at his papers. He told her they were called maps. Amy turned around and called him. "What is that?" she asked, pointing to his vehicle.

"It's a type of cycle. In the past, many people used this type of machine to get around, I...." The man stopped as he noticed Amy with her head down. "What's wrong?" She looked up with tears running down her cheek.

"If the Clouds have done what they have done, then why did you come for me? WHY?" More tears began to flow.

With a caring face, the man got up and sat down next to her. He took her hand. "I took you away from that place because I need your help."

Amy, her face now red because of the tears, stared at the man. "What?"

The man hesitated as if he were unsure whether or not to tell her. Then he looked her in the eyes. "I need to find out more about the 'Clouds' as you call them. I want to try to enter one."

Amy's eyes widened, "Only prophets can enter the Clouds...."

The man interrupted, "Or someone bearing the mark." Amy ran her fingers over the mark.

She was quiet as they continued their journey. At one point, the vehicle stopped. "We have to walk now to save up on fuel," the man said as he got off the vehicle. Amy followed. She stayed close to the man as he pushed the vehicle along. Dark clouds began to form over them. Soon rain began to fall. He stopped to dig a large jacket out of one of the sacks, which she held over her head.

Soon the path they were on began to get muddy, and Amy had a hard time keeping up. At one point, the vehicle got stuck, and the man called on her to help. She threw the jacket into the side cart and helped him push the vehicle out of the mud. As the sky darkened even more, she realized that night was coming on. Not long after that, her legs finally began give out on her, so the man found a place to rest under a large rock out-cropping. He even got a fire going with a small, strange device. Amy watched as he held it down to the wood and with the flick of his thumb, a flame shot out, setting the wood on fire. When the fire was going well, he held it up so Amy could take a closer look. "It's called a lighter," he said with a smile on his face. As they warmed and dried themselves by the fire, the man threw Amy a tan packet and told her to open it. As she did, he opened one of his own. She saw many strange looking items. "This is food," he said as he took a shiny looking rectangle from his packet and opened it, revealing something that seemed to be made of wheat. He began to eat it. Amy found a similar item in her packet. It was a strange meal, but it satisfied her hunger. After they finished off everything that was in the packets, he rolled out the bedroll on the ground and handed her a small pillow. "You can sleep on this side," he said. Amy lay down, and he covered her with his patchwork coat. He stretched out on the other side with his back to her.

As Amy looked up at the stars, she asked, "Would you have still taken me from the village if I didn't have this mark—if it was someone else who was chosen to be a new prophet?"

At first the man didn't answer her. Then he said, "There were other reasons to take you." Soon she could tell by his breathing that he was asleep.

Turning on her side, Amy noticed something in his coat. She took it out and looked at it in the firelight. It was a picture of the woman from the image he showed her. Amy put the picture back. "Why did he have a picture of my mother?" she thought to herself as she went to sleep.

The next day they continued on their journey. The sky began

to clear, and Amy could see that they were heading toward some mountains overlooking a valley. As the clouds parted, she noticed something floating above the mountains. Her eyes widened as she realized it was an Iron Cloud. She could see strange lights from it shining down on the hills and into the valleys. "I never saw one this close before."

The man stared straight ahead as he said, "It's going to get a lot closer." He then turned one of the handle bars to make the vehicle go faster. Their vehicle sped toward the base of a mountain, where they quickly got off and hiked up its side. Amy noticed the man was now holding the rifle-like weapon she saw on the vehicle and was also carrying a large satchel. She also noticed he seemed to be getting more nervous as they approached the top.

"What's wrong?" she asked.

The man hesitated then said, "We're about to do something that has never been done before. I'm not sure if this will work."

Amy's eyes widened as they reached the top. The Iron Cloud blocked out the sky above them. "Quick!" the man said, "Give me your arm." She held it out to him. Almost frantically, he pushed back the sleeve of the oversized jacket, revealing the mark on her arm. "Hold it up to the machine. Quickly!" he said as the green lights began to move toward them. Amy took a deep breath and did as he told her. The green lights played over their bodies. They covered their eyes as the man held his rifle close. Then the lights focused on the mark on Amy's arm. Suddenly, they went out. They had just a moment to look around before the Iron Cloud began to light up the sky, and an octagonal-shaped object came down from the cloud and landed next to them. They exchanged questioning glances before moving closer to examine the object. Then she remembered Prophet Turner telling her that a "servant" would come for her. "I think we're supposed to get on it," she said and stepped cautiously onto the machine. The man hesitated for a moment then joined her. The octagonal object lifted off the ground and headed towards the Cloud. Amy and the man stared in amazement as the object entered the Cloud through an opening in its underbelly.

They found themselves standing in the middle of a dark area. The man pulled out a long, rod-like device from his bag. He shook it up and down a few times before pushing a button on the side. A light beamed out from it. Even with the light, it was hard for them to tell where they were. Suddenly, the area lit up, and they realized they were standing in the middle of a wide, long, curving hallway. The man turned off his light and put it away as they looked up and down the corridor, wondering which way to go. Then lights in the floor came on leading in one direction down the hall. Amy noticed there were long rods that covered the ceiling running down the corridor's length. They followed the lights until they came to a large room. In the room, there was an odd-looking podium with an octagon at the top of it. As they approached it, they could see rectangular buttons with strange images on them.

"I think they're letters," the man said as he touched one. But nothing happened. Amy then pressed a large red one at the top of the octagon, and a screen appeared on the wall. On the screen were more of the strange letters and symbols. They moved around in a circle looking at the chart. Amy touched another one of the symbols, and the screen changed to an image of a large room with unusual beds with weird arm-like devices and machines attached to them. She touched another symbol and saw some sort of storage room with several oblong-shaped machines resting on top of each other.

"See if you can find a schematic of the ship," the man said. Amy looked at him bewildered. "A drawing, a plan. Something that shows how the ship works." She pressed one, and a skeletal image of the ship appeared. In certain areas, there were little octagons with more of the strange symbols in them. Amy noticed a bar at the bottom of the octagon. She moved her hand across it and saw that it highlighted different octagons. "Try that one there," the man said as he pointed to a octagon in the center of the ship. Amy highlighted it.

"I wonder how...." Amy interrupted the man as she touched the bar again causing a room to come up on the screen. There was a large tower-like device in its center. The man noticed how several lines ran from the other octagons to that one room, and the lines came up to the device in it.

While the man pondered his next move, Amy stared at the

images in wondermeant, having never seen such things before in her life. "Amy, I want you to go back to the area where we came from and wait there for me." The tone in his voice was very stern.

"Why?" Amy asked, as she turned to the man.

"It's nothing. Just go back to the room and wait for me there," he said in the same stern tone.

"What's going on?" Amy demanded.

The man then reached into his bag and pulled out a large block with some sort of device on it. "This is a bomb. I have a couple more just like it. I'm going to that room on the screen and use them to try and knock out this machine." Amy tried her best to follow what the man was saying. "If that does what I think it does, then I might have a chance to destroy or at least damage this thing."

"But you said…."

The man interrupted her. "Yes, I know. But no one has ever gotten this far before. I have to take a chance." The man then began to look around the room to try and figure out how he could get there. He noticed what looked like a vent on the wall and looked back at the screen. "That might be what I'm looking for," the man said, walking away from the podium toward the wall. The vent was high and out of reach of the man.

"I can help. Please let me," she said as she joined him.

The man looked up at the vent and then at Amy. "Okay, just stay close to me and do exactly what I say. Understand?" Amy nodded her head in agreement.

"I think you can pull it off. Here, let me see if I can lift you up there." He strained as he held Amy near it. She pulled at the vent a few times before it came loose and dropped to the floor. She saw that there was a shaft behind the vent. The shaft was long and dark. She pulled herself up into it, and reached down to help the man up. That accomplished, he pointed his rifle forward and, with his other hand, got out his light and turned it on again. He shined it down the shaft. They could just make out pipes that were running over their heads down its length. "Come on, but be careful," he said.

They crawled for what seemed like ages. Finally, they got to another vent at the end of the shaft. Together they looked through the slats. On the other side there was an immense room. In its center was a structure with a huge, blue, diamond-like crystal. Amy began to push at the vent. "What are you doing?" he asked as the vent fell to the floor below.

"What?" She exclaimed, as a strange egg shaped device flew up toward the now open shaft. Amy watched as it opened up, and a weapon appeared from it. The man pointed his rifle at it and pulled the trigger. A beam shot out from the rifle. It hit the object dead center. In a spark of light and smoke the device exploded, falling to the floor. "What was that?" Amy exclaimed.

"Must have been a sentry to protect this room. Hurry, there'll probably be more," he said as they lowered themselves down from the vent to the floor.

"What is that thing you were using? I've never seen anything like it."

The man looked at his rifle. "You mean this? It's made from bits of these machines like the one I just shot. Now, come on, let's get over to that device." He pointed toward the tower-like structure in the center of the room. They had to move over several large pipes that ran from the floor to the structure. Amy noticed that several of the pipes ran all the way up to the walls of the room and into them. The man reached into his sack and pulled out one of his bombs and looked around the structure. When he found what he thought was a likely spot, he placed the first bomb there. He and Amy then made their way around the structure placing the other bombs as best they could.

"Come on! Let's get out of here!" Just then several more of those strange devices began to appear near the structure, and a large octagon-shaped door opened up, and an oblong machine came flying out of it and joined the devices. Weapons emerged from all of them. "Run!" the man yelled as he headed towards the vent opening. They clambered over the pipes as a beam just missed Amy's arm, singeing the sleeve of her jacket. The man almost threw Amy up to the vent, then turned and fired his rifle at the devices as they began to close in on them. The beam cut into several of them at the same time, causing them to explode.

Amy looked out the vent and down at the old man. "Give me your hand!" she yelled down to him.

He looked up as his rifle began to recharge. "Go! I'll be all right." A beam hit the area beneath Amy. "Just go!" he yelled.

Reluctantly, Amy turned away as the man continued to fight the devices. Amy crawled down the shaft. Since she didn't have the man's light, she had to feel her way. As everything began to shake violently, Amy looked back and saw a fire was coming up the shaft. Pipes around her began to break, and the fire grew closer. Just then the shaft broke apart, and Amy began a long fall.

The debris of the machine covered the hills and mountain. Some of it was still on fire as a man and a woman came out of a cave near the mountain where the Iron Cloud fell. The man was tall, and he and the woman were wearing coats similar to what the old man, her friend, wore. "I don't believe it! The old man did it!" the man said as he looked around. They began to search the wreckage to see if they could find anything useful. The woman came across a large, undamaged piece of the machine near the base of the mountain and was shocked to find a young woman lying beside it. The woman called out to the man who was looking at the remains of one of the egg-shaped devices. He dropped it and joined her. The girl's face and clothes were blackened from the blast, but she was beginning to show signs of life.

"Don't move," the woman told her, and she began to check Amy's body for injuries. As the man came over he noticed the mark on Amy's arm. "Is she a leader?" he said as he pointed to it.

"Of course, how do you think the old man got into that machine? Wait! I think I know who this is. Go get the medical supplies. Go!" While the man went back to the cave, the woman knelt down next to her. "Is your name Amy?" Amy nodded her head slightly. "Were you with an old man in that machine."

"Yes," Amy said as she felt her strength coming back. Although there were bruises and cuts on her body, she was aware of no major injures.

When the man returned, Amy was sitting up, leaning against a piece of the machine. As the woman tended a cut on Amy's arm, the girl kept her eyes on the strange marks on the man's face. "What?" the man said, not knowing what she was staring at.

"I think she's looking at your face, Stitch."

"These?" He asked as he ran his hand across the stitch marks.

"His name is Daric Johnson, but everyone calls him Stitch. My name is Rebecca Roop. I can't believe you survived all of this. Your grandfather told me about his plan. I didn't think it would work, let alone actually bring down the machine…" Amy ceased to pay attention as Rebecca continued to talk. She just looked off into the distance and wondered about her mother.

As the sun set on the village, Amy's mother stood in her daughter's room. Prophet Turner stood behind her with another of the other prophets. He looked at her strangely. "I'm sorry. We've checked everywhere we could, but we couldn't find Amy. We can only hope that she's okay." He and the other prophet then turned and left.

The mother looked out the window and quietly said to herself, "Great Cloud, please watch over my daughter." She then turned from the window and put out the light in Amy's room.

ANN NICHOLSON TAIT's life's work has involved various forms of visual arts, graphics, painting, pottery, sculpture, quilting and other crafts. A native of Pennsylvania, Ann moved to Brevard in 1996 and began writing in 1997. She is currently working on a historical murder mystery novel called *Black November*. Ann produced the Transylvania Writers' Alliance's first book, *Mountain Moods and Moments*, preparing the manuscript, doing the layout, the cover, and the illustrations. She is the illustrator and cover designer for this publication.

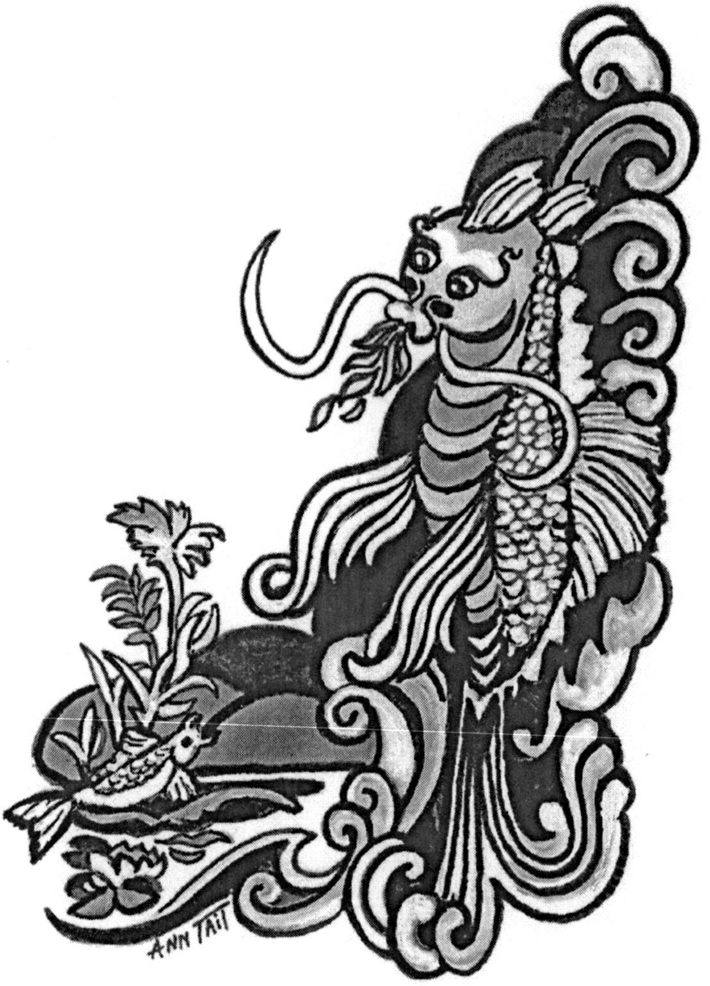
ANN TAIT

A FISH TALE

A short story in rhyme
(Nishikigoi - (Ney-she-key-goy) - Japanese for Koi - ornamental Carp)

The dawn sun beats on the water's surface,
   As lilies open their petals in lust for light.
Iris and grasses stretch upward with zeal and grace.
Dragonflies and Damselflies awaken and take flight.

Beneath swaying aqua plants, sparkling fish flow
   to the top of the pool, circling in glittering rings.
A frog leaps from lily pad, startled by a swooping crow,
   as the breeze blows flowers' scents and a bird sings.

It's morning in a Japanese garden a long time ago.
   Standing on a bridge, is an old man named Yoshu.
He watches his beautiful fish flutter in a splendorous glow.
   The waterfall splashes into the lily pond of zircon blue.

Seeing Yoshu's reflection, the Koi quickly appear.
   They know each other well. The fish do not fear or flee.
   His glittering treasures approach him very near.
   Nishikigoi and Yoshu; fish and man in harmony.

Yoshu comes with food at morning's early light,
   He stands in the grass where water meets land,
He tosses food high, for fish to catch in leaping flight.
   At dusk he touches his fish, feeding them from hand.

Yoshu's mind wanders back fifty years to his Chinese wife.
   After three years of married bliss, Mai Li passed on.
Now he watches Kohaku, her Koi, which carries her spirit life.
   In grief, he locked his gate and lives aloof, mourning this wrong.

The union of Yoshu and Mai Li was met with much disdain.

They broke the rules of racial restriction and family tradition.
Their love could not defeat the shunning and society's refrain.
The world thought Mai Li's death was the Gods' retribution.

Yoshu spots each fish, speaking their names in his head.
Sumi, black koi was in the pond when he was a boy.
They are his many colored jewels; blue and gold and red.
Lost of any human friends, the fish are his only joy.

He has fish of lapis and garnet on shining scales of pearl.
Mai Li's Kohaku, brought from China, white and scarlet bright.
Gold, silver, copper and bronze metallic marvels swirl.
Shiro white, ki yellow, Orenji orange, gemstones in the light.

Yoshu shivers with chill as he notices an ominous sky.
"Tanchos, show me your red crowns, hurry, please come."
They swim toward him, clearing the surface, as if to ask him "why."
He says, "Royals, watch the kingdom, my time is almost done."

Sun down, day is gone.
Old man sighs and then he dies.
Garden has no song.

Koi lose will to leap.
Spring day turns, November gray.
Sad Nishikigoi weep.

It's morning in the garden, the pond is very still.
The birds sing no song, the frog is silent on his leaf.
The Koi aren't swimming playfully; sadness takes their will.
Lily petals closed tight, the grasses bow in grief.

Suddenly there's a flashing splashing of red and white.
Mai Li's Kohaku is frantically leaping up the waterfall.
She knows there are strong rapids ahead that she must fight,
to fill her Chinese destiny. She hears the ancient call.

Chinese legend says, koi who dare to climb the waterfall
and challenge the wild rapids, will reach the pool of purity.
The Koi that proves its worthiness, and answers the special call,
becomes a good dragon and provider of all the Koi's security.

Sun soul, chosen one.
Woman's spirit enters Koi,
Koi becomes dragon.

Good dragon blessed
old man's Koi and water joy,
Spring smiles, old man rests.

YELLOW

The Dutchman lived in the south of France
in a four room house
...of *yellow*.

By day he sat under the blazing sun
...of *yellow*.
He painted in a pensive trance, then with zeal,
cornfields and sunflowers, sienna and ochre
for hours upon hours
...all *yellow*.

When days were gray and shadowed
... the *yellow*,
he sauntered alone, sluggish and sullen,
searching of sense, while sinking in sorrow,
stumbling in gray while seeking
...some *yellow*.

A straw hat always on his head,
slumped upon prickly brows,
stained fingers stroked his beard of red.

Strained fingers forced the bristled brush,
across canvas in erratic rush,
as his green eyes flashed with flecks
...of *yellow.*

By night, in pubs lanterns' beaming light
he painted tavern fights with furor and power;
he painted brothel girls and starry night
in whirling swirls of cobalt, cerulean
...and *yellow.*

Before the dawn discharged the dark,
he staggered to his house
...of *yellow.*

Not yet dead, but seized with dread,
he rolled into his bed, curling in a ball,
sleeping like a naked armadillo,
lacking safety of a shell,
doomed to exist in painted hell,
lost in his world
...of *yellow.*

BREAKER MONSTER

Excerpt from Black November, a novel in process.

    Twelve-year-old Arnie was hunched over, wrapped in a heavy quilt, hugging himself against the cold of the day and the cold of trepidation. It was overcast, the air thick with snow. Hilda and Robby watched their older brother through the kitchen window as the heavy snow covered the design on the quilt, causing the boy to appear to be a snowdrift upon the bench. Robby snickered and called his brother a snow ghost.
    Arnie loved the spot his mother called her "chapel." Arnie's father had built the bench, covered by a trellis, and had encased

the little garden with a white picket fence. Elsa liked to sit there, absorbing the fragrance of her flowers, while being soothed by the bubbly sounds of the nearby creek that ran parallel to the property line. It was Elsa's haven to escape from the dreariness of everyday life in Carbonville.

Elsa's garden was also special to Arnie. He particularly liked it in the midsummer when both perennials and annuals were in bloom. He liked the "climbers," the clematis and morning glories, because they formed walls - walls to close in the beauty of the garden and close out the coal gray that plagued the village. The bright pink roses that climbed the trellis above the bench grew thick and hung down like bunches of grapes. The faces on the pansies amused him. He marveled at the hummingbirds spearing the hollyhocks. This was the private place Arnie came to think, to dream, to pretend and to cry.

The boy solemnly looked to the west, wishing for a sunset, wishing for this day to end. There was a glow, but it was not a sunset. It was the red hue of the beehive ovens burning high-grade coal to make coke to be used in the steel industry. Even the heavy snow could not veil the toxic coal tar gas smell that draped over the village.

He remembered the horrible smell that came from the shaft this morning. Now he knew what the odor was. It was the smell of the unidentified burned body that the foreman found in the mine.

Arnie turned his head slightly to the south and could see the outline of the blackened wooden structure called The Breaker. Two-thirds of the building was long and seemed low at 30 feet, in contrast to the other third of the structure that jutted out in unlikely angles, rising to a height of 90 feet. It loomed dark, threatening, and ugly above the rows of tiny company houses below. The Breaker's odd lines drew a silhouette that Arnie likened to that of a vicious carnivorous monster.

Day after day, car after car loaded with hunks of coal were pulled out of the depths of the mine. The cars screeched as they were pulled by cable up an incline path to the top of the Breaker, where laborers shoveled the coal down chutes. The lumps tumbled into giant steel teeth that were mounted on cylinders, where they were crunched into smaller pieces.

The coal was then poured into a series of screens and sifted, separating it into categories by size.

Arnie stared at the ominous building that he called "Breaker Monster," remembering the scary stories he told the younger kids; about how the monster grinds its massive jaws as it chews the coal with its huge sharp teeth. He told them that it spewed deadly smoke that ravaged the trees and robbed the grass of its green. He said it chomped coal and then spit piles of dust that blackened the bodies and souls of the mules and the men. Arnie smirked as he said, "The monster swallowed the coal into its filthy acid stomach, digested it and expelled it into piles of poop." He informed the kids that their houses were heated with "monster crap."

Arnie's own stomach turned in revulsion, realizing that just a few years ago, boys from age ten to fourteen were put into the lower part of the breaker building, into a squat, dark room, which was at a forty-five degree angle. Usually four "breaker boys," also called "slate pickers," were placed at either side of the machines to pick out the slate and stone as it tumbled past them from screen to screen. With aching backs, cut fingers, and lungs filled with black dust, they worked twelve hours a day. They toiled in rooms polluted with sulfuric acid, cramped in a damp, dark space that was too low for even a small boy to stand. The boys started as slate pickers, moving up with age to other arduous jobs.

Finally, if they lived that long, they became "real miners," with the likelihood of being burned or crippled at some point in their lives, and doomed to "miner's asthma," also known as "Black Lung."

With much stubborn resistance, Old Man Welborn, the mine owner, had finally been forced by child labor laws to install machinery to help sort the coal. The laws stated that a boy had to be fourteen to work in the breaker and sixteen to work in the mines. Welborn still found ways to get away with paying low wages, by hiring disabled miners to do the jobs once done by the ten to fourteen-year-olds.

Arnie glanced back to the coke ovens burning orange, trying

to imagine what a burned body looked like and, at the same time, trying not to imagine it.

He turned toward the frozen Horseshoe Creek. He longed for summer, for the colors and sweet scents of flowers. He needed sounds other than chugging trains, clapping hooves, and that damned whistle. The shift whistle. The death whistle. He needed the creek to thaw so he could hear it bubble. He needed to hear chirping birds and crickets. God, how he needed summer. He needed to grow up so he could leave Carbonville.

DAYBREAK CANVAS
(Lake Jordan, North Carolina)

Slow breezes caress shades of summer greens.
The beach is quiet and deserted
except for one egret and me.
Small black shells splatter brown sand.
Weather-sculpted tree root gnomes
huddle in clans.
The sun, cut into slivers by
dense trees---lazily rises.

The lake is content,
surrounded by its forest fortress.
Silver waters with reflections of viridian
sway gracefully with the current,
depositing foamy designs on the shoreline.
I ingest the peace and solitude.
If for only a moment, nature's painting
belongs to me alone.
I hang it in the art gallery of my mind.

As the sun rises and warms,
creatures awaken and stir.
The forest speaks, the water whispers,
as the wind tells secrets to those who listen.
Dawn unveils a masterpiece.

NOSTALGIA ON TIMES SQUARE

The combo plays the song that Mingus wrote.
I listen and I see the city in the notes.
Kids on the street, cops on the beat.
Artists sketching, Poodles stretching,
The rustling, restless avenues.
Honking, shouting, quiet conversation.
Silent, solemn souls... just roaming.

A fancy lady steps across a man
swaddled in a soiled coat,
curled on the walk.

Busy people going places...
plays, restaurants, meetings.

Rushing here and there.
Star searching, self-searching
...searching.
Busy people going nowhere.
Beggars, players, slayers,
bookers, hookers, on-lookers.

Tourists in awe of this place,
of multiple races and unusual faces.
Street musicians strumming,
blowing, singing,
for indifferent ears and no cheers.
Actors waiting on tables,
filled with actors waiting.

Schizophrenics screaming,
"End of the world!"
Street preachers preaching,

"Christ is coming. "
I listen with closed eyes
and smell the city.
Gasoline, sweat, life, death,
flowers for six bucks a bunch.
And hot dogs for lunch,
all in the city's breath.

New Yorkers seize Manhattan.
Tourists embrace Manhattan.
Jazz players, artists, and poets
...dwell in the nostalgia.

SAXOPHONE

Moan, saxophone.
Cry.
Open my soul.
Notes creep
into my veins,
through my heart,
beating the beat.

Notes seep,
to the ruler of my pain,
to my brain.
An influx of
musical endorphins.

Purr, saxophone,
through the gray,
to the gray matter.
Stimulate the serotonin.
Make my heat stop moanin'.

Laugh, saxophone!

NEW BLUE TRICYCLE

The American woman pauses on the winding stair to her rented Mexican Palupa, and watches a small Mayan girl named Thalia whirl the wheels of her new blue tricycle. She rides in circles in the tiny courtyard behind her family's faded pink, stucco house. A cement wall topped with upward thrusting jagged broken bottles encloses it. The child wears a soiled flowered dress that is pulled across the bicycle seat exposing her bare behind. Her feet are stuffed into the toes of her mother's Sunday high heels. Her raven hair dangles from a frayed red ribbon. The high heels drag along the cracked cement, etching lines into the topping of sand and dried mud. There is no grass. One Jasmine vine climbs along the wall. Thalia sings, her large brown eyes sparkling, lost in her imagination, oblivious to her poverty. A thin, raggedy, yellow dog opens heavy eyelids and rises from his corner in the shade to observe this new moving object, then flops back into his dazed world of sameness.

At the Plaza Las Glorias, a plush tourist hotel about a half mile away, Thalia's mother scrubs the hard tile floor around a pair of king-sized beds and pictures the worn hammocks that hang in her two room house. She has never slept in a bed.

Thalia's father proudly watches his little girl from an open window. He doesn't notice the lime-colored lizard that brushes his arm as it dashes though the opening and streaks across the cement floor, disappearing into the clutter that fills the room. The father smiles as he imagines his wife secretly hiding pesos in her bible for many months to save for the tricycle. Then he sighs; he has no job, no car, no beds, but his daughter has her new blue bike. He is grateful. His thoughts are interrupted by the sound of rattling wheels and the deep-toned ring of the bell of the "Agua Man" pushing his wooden cart along the pot-holed street, laden with 25-gallon jugs of fresh water. The yellow dog lifts his head and lets out a halfhearted bark as the father goes out to the street to buy water. "*Hola Paco, Como estas? Una botella.*"

"*Bien, gracias,*" Paco chuckles, as he lifts the heavy jug from his cart. The greeting seldom changes, because life seldom changes.

The old man, toothless, grins and says, "*Hasta luego.*" Paco plods on like an old plow horse.

Thalia suddenly notices the American woman watching her. The three-year-old waves, happily showing off her new bike. Shedding her mother's shoes, she peddles faster with her tough little brown feet, as she rides to nowhere. Smiling, she waves and says, "*Bonito triciclo.*" Thalia will accept her lot in life and find joy in small things. It is the Mayan way. Perhaps it is a better way

NIGHT WRITER'S INSOMNIA

We, of foreshortened dreams
and awake nightmares, in starless stark,
roam the possessed opaque dark,
in lacey gowns, leather, rags and jeans.

With hearts, minds, eyes in strain,
faltering feet stumble in exhaustion.
We search for viable inspiration
to entice, create, to purge the pain.

We lust for love, possessions and success;
thus we must persist one more time,
step by step, day by day, line by line,
by luck, by whim, by skillful doggedness.

We yawn, yearn, scream for slumber,
yet resist the sleep, lest we fail to spot
that one magic word, or moment, or thought,
in fear that needed rest will put us under.

THE LANDSCAPE OF HIS LINES

My father wrote a legacy for me

and my children to share and see.
He wrote his worth and essence
and left his very presence
in his prose and rhymes.

He bound his words in books so we
could wander through
the landscape of his lines.

I find myself exploring the caverns of his soul.
I stumble on stones of satire, as I begin to stroll
down youthful paths and trails of time.
I roam in rocky romance and leap in love sublime.

I grope my way through days of gloom,
and then find wit in his humor room.
I adventurously balance on his legend logs,
recalling bedtime tales, where Annie chases frogs.

I see Dad's reflection in a pool of tears
that trickle through memories of our years.
His joyful words are blazed in light.
His sorrows, shadow like the night.

His terms of truth are oak tree towers.
His tender texts are summer flowers.
He reads aloud to me, but no one else can hear.
When I look upon a book, my Dad is always near.

ELIZABETH OWEN TAYLOR was born just outside Philadelphia but is a lifelong resident of Western North Carolina. After earning a baccalaureate and master's degrees from Wake Forest University, she taught freshman and sophomore English at Brevard College for four years, always requiring students to write haikus, sonnets, and other forms, but writing none herself. Following a hiatus of many years, she is now an eager producer of verse.

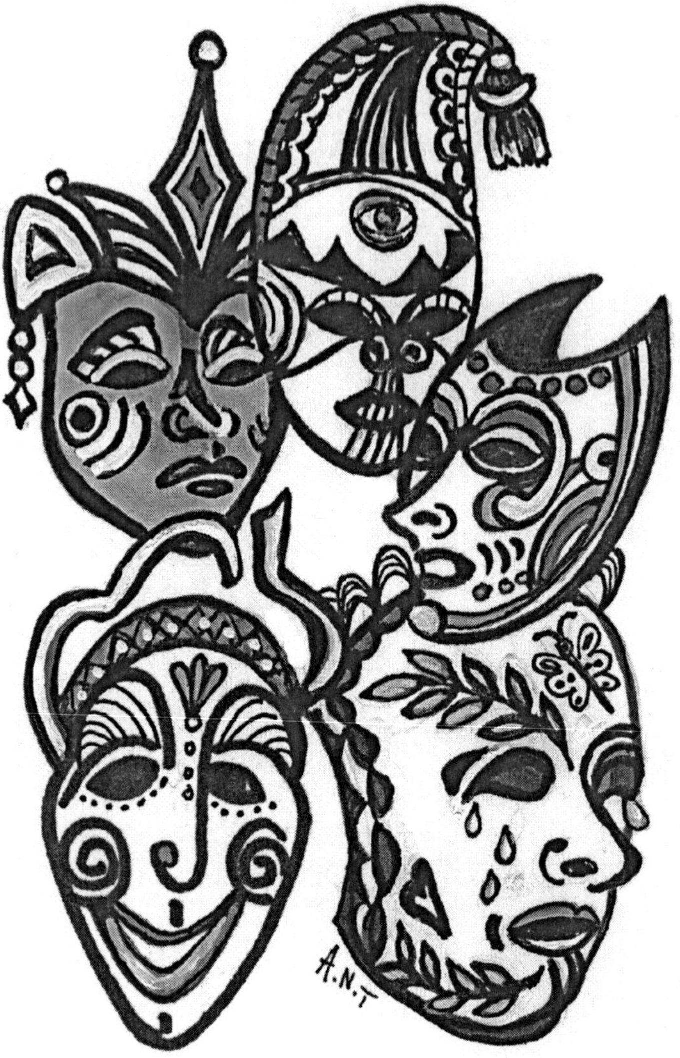
A.N.T

THE FORMER STOIC

She entrapped herself
in a cage of convention.
She wore masks.
She thought everyone
wore masks.
She stored hers
sorted on shelves.

She sought nothing,
Not to be disappointed.
She nurtured a stone
In her chest
Near her heart.
She required resurrection.

Ask and it shall be given you.

THE END OF INNOCENCE

Last week we met again since years asunder
And spoke with joy of well-remembered wonder.
I learned to ride a bike by riding hers;
We shared a love of mangy, common curs.

She said I told her once, "No Santa Claus."
This piece of information gave her pause.
She asked me how I knew with such a look
That I retorted quickly, "From a book."

Strange how I had of this no memory,
But she had strained to maintain normalcy.

ERIN'S SONNET

From infancy you stole our hearts,
Alert and lively in all your parts,
Winsome and graceful in every way,
Unfettered and elfin in joyful play.

Frogs and bogs were your delight:
Nothing it seemed could cause you fright.
To shores and jungles you ventured afar.
No hurdle blocked you from reaching your star.

On stage you were lovely, a long-legged queen,
Mostly in motion, but sometimes serene.
When you gave vent to choreography,
We wondered whither your biology?

Then straight to Manhattan to test the boards.
You bear our blessings and hopes for rewards.

FIRST KISSES

When I was young and slender as a limb,
Ambrosia was in season just with him.
The loamy smell of spring would plunge us madly
Into kisses deep and long,
Enough to slake a thirst so vast
It scarce could be explained.
Entwined, we leaned against a great tree trunk.
All time stood still
As we elixir drunk.
All else forgot
And we alone remained.

SERENDIPITY

*(stumbling quite unexpectedly
upon something quite wonderful)*

She disliked cats;
His cat was named Raleigh.
She had a place to rent;
He needed shelter.
She had a fireplace;
He liked a fire in winter.
She had a player piano;
He liked music.
She had a garden;
He liked to dig.
She had traveled abroad;
He once lived in England.
She had a smile to beguile;
He had a lingering laugh.
She had a flair for fashion;
He had a way with words.
Their hair color blended;
Their dance steps matched.
She could read his mind;
He could guess her thoughts.
She grew a tolerance for cats;
He formed a fondness for landlords.
She counted books in a library;
He counted money in a bank;
The neighbors counted a couple.
Gloria in excelsis Deo.

Update: *In August 2003 Raleigh the cat died
at the ripe age of fourteen, deeply mourned
by the couple's triplets: Sarah, Hope, and John.*

VALENTINE'S DAY

Roses are red.
Violets are blue.
Could you be true,
You would dance in my head.

If roses are red,
And violets are blue,
Could you be true,
I would come to your bed.

As roses are red,
And violets are blue,
Could you be true,
Then we would be wed.

Since roses are red,
And violets are blue,
But you can't be true,
Then you'll not be fed.

NIGHT TRAIN TO ST. PETERSBURG

Hurtling through the Russian
Night on silken rails
Where flashing hooves once
Drew imperial sleighs,
The two estranged
Joined in darkness deep,
And coupling spawned its
Splendid mystery.
Spirits soared, memory seared
In carnal celebration,
But…no beginning,
No renewal, only ending.

THE BEGINNING OF WISDOM

("In the middle of the road of my life
I awoke in a dark wood where
The true way was wholly lost."
Opening lines of Dante's Divine Comedy)

Of course I know what baby owls look like.
That summer in St. Louis with our tyke
I saw a dozen owls, quite young, displayed,
Unblinking eyes like 'gators in the shade.

The dreams came later after many years;
Midsummer found me captive to my fears.
I read a tale of someone else's dream
And realized my own twice raised a theme.

Deep in the woods I held a light in hand.
The beams struck hard against the darkened land.
At once an owlet's gaze peered forth, a seerlet,
Athena laughed. Her symbol wise did leerlet,

Not in the full blown majesty of truth,
But infant wisdom for the pilgrim sooth.

DREAM QUESTS

Briskly the dreamer strides
Along endless corridors
Framed by locked doors;
Climbs serial stairways
Spiraling nowhere,
Races through labyrinths
Of underground warrens dimly lit;

Distractedly rushing,
Seeking, searching,
No solace, no respite, no exit.

Resolutely the dreamer clambers
Up a steep, rocky trail,
Towering cliffs to the left,
Sheer precipice to the right.
A careless stumble arcs
Pebbles into emptiness.
Looming in the distance,
A well-known citadel beckons,
Its skyline distinctive.
Alluring summit
Eludes the climber.
Ascent is all.

Wearily the dreamer wanders
Through numberless doorways
Of drab tenement houses,
Colorless and thick with dust.
Long habitation
Prompts exploration
Of well-hidden rooms.
At the heart of one hovel
The dreamer discovers
A single large chamber,
Lit by blazing torches,
Furnished with tables
Of burnished wood,
Ottomans of cordovan leather,
Carpets of paisley pattern,
Bedding of silken damask.
Revelation.
Exhilaration.
Seek and ye shall find.

SEIZE THE RIPENESS

Bereft of beauty, youth, and slenderness,
She views all things with new-eyed wariness.
Invisible, she can perfect her gaze,
Observe the world around her, trace the maze
Of real life, engaged but looser linked,
No longer drowned in hormones or instinct,
But fitly philosophical,
Rejoicing in the comical.

A DISTINCTION

No perfection in this world,
Sages teach: not so.
In music, cats, and colors
There is perfection.
There is no permanence.
Even mountains move in time:
Rising, sinking, eroding, exploding.

ONE SEPTEMBER MORNING
(9. 11. 2001)

Autumn in New York
Blighted by plunging towers.
Complacency squelched.

Twin towers so tall
Collapse in cascades of death.
All ash and ruin.

Customary creeds

Out of Our Hearts and Minds

Momentarily at loss.
Comprehension numbed.

All Americans
New Yorkers for a season,
Transcending horror.

Pennsylvania.
One passenger cries, "Let's roll."
The sacrifice dive.

Pentagon agape,
Stalwart military heart
Breached by civil craft.

Air transportation,
Money markets, government
All stilled one morning.

Ubiquitous flags.
Acclamation for heroes.
United we stand.

DAILY SPECTACLES

With glacial speed
The evening sky kaleidoscopes
From daylight to dark
In measured degrees:
azure,
periwinkle,

After flamingos and lemons of sunset
The blueing of night is splendor serene.

Before break of dawn
Darkness brightens in reverse.
Sometimes I see it.

THE ORGY

Not once have I beheld a burning bush,
But summer served a teeming bush at noon.
Instead of bees extracting nectar neat
From purple trumpet blossoms pollen full,
Inspection counted scores of beetles green,
Those iridescent insects from Japan
Intent upon the very force of fusion
and keenly bound in frenzied coupling fast.

Not birds, nor bees, but beetles besotted
Proclaimed in conjunction instinctual bliss.
By ardor absorbed, these beetles conjoined
Attracted only me. None other paused
Nor marked their tangible labor of love
Excepting their Maker most glorious,
And in submission to His purpose plain
They went about their procreative task.

Holy Creator of insects and men
Commands us to be fruitful in our time.
Adoration sanctifies vocation
And re-creation is our Maker's will.
"In imitation of His example
And in obedience to His command"
We earthly alchemists strain art from life,
Distilling timelessness from temporality.

SEASONAL SENSORIES

Spring greening quickens
Vision; moist mulch smells engulf.
Sight and scent converge.

Against tall dark trees
A curtain of twinkling lights:
Flirtatious fireflies.

Just dull bugs by day,
Mating games transform them to
Small strobe lights by night.

Summer solstice spills
Over with incessant rasps
Of insect queries.

Monarchs winging south,
Skies cloudless blue, air clear sharp,
Leaves spiraling down.

Crisp crunch underfoot,
Woodlands exploding color,
Leaf-looker season.

Deep winter silence.
Dormant life and quiescence.
Dark stillness lingers.

Spring's aura shimmers,
Radiates luminescence.
Chlorophyll trumps all.

HOMAGE TO BARE TREES

Distant stands lace the ridges
With woody filigree
Of delicate clarity.
Solitary sentinels,
Deftly sculpted skeletons,
Display a vascular silhouette:
From trunk to twig
Diameters diminish
As branchings increase,
Mating strength to elegance,
Engendering naked grace.
Meanwhile moths mock
The patterns and palettes of bark,
Claiming the refuge of neutrals,
Claiming the solace of neutrals,
Praise be.

ANTHONY TINSLEY grew up in Transylvania's Cathey's Creek area, where—since splitting from the Big Easy—he's lived now again for about seven years. Four of his poems have been published, and he has many multiples of that number of rejection letters pinned to his bedroom wall. He vacations rarely, reads voraciously and is passionate about politics. "I look forward to the downfall of American fascism," he says, "and to the election of the next Democratic president."

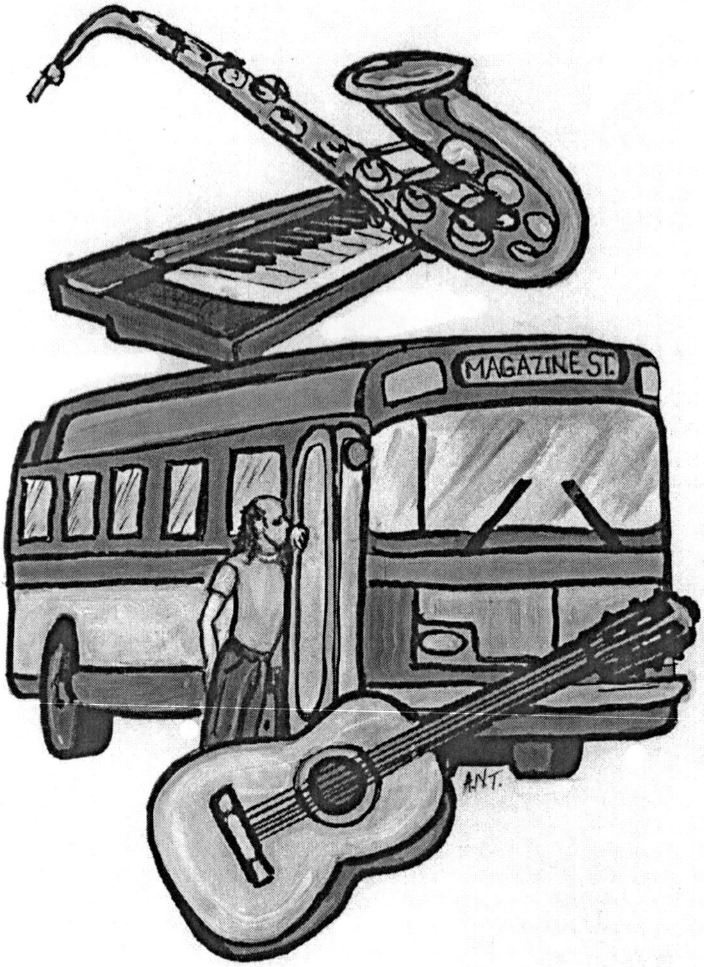
MAGAZINE ST.
A.N.T.

CHURNING

She must have known
Her grandson had good ears.
Not that he could hear great distance
Then he would be a hunter, like his father
Or her husband. But just that rhythm
(to which she was accustomed)
Would frighten his infant ears so much
His wail would echo all through Walnut Holler.
She took him in her lap
He calmed down a bit.
He might be a musician some day,
His ears were that sensitive.
The milk wasn't butter yet,
But her grandson was secure
In grandmaternal arms.

PAPA

On the way to work
On the Magazine bus
Early enough for me to get a seat.
Past Lee who looms
Over his circle this dreary
Morning with his back to me,
I recall an image long lost
To me though preserved
In whichever drawer Grandma
Keeps her pictures.
My father's father with a Gillespie
Rifle gun, sighting down
It, shooting the damned thing
(an explosion, childhood fear).
Heading toward my stop I think he

Never turned his back either.
He stood face to face
With the cancer that killed him.
Walking toward the office
Wet-eyed, proud
Of that but glad it's still dark,
I reflect that he never really understood me,
Didn't get that his first born's first born
Didn't want to learn to fish or rabbit hunt.
One day when I was about
Fifteen, he looked at me from his chair
And said, "It ain't right, Anth'ny, that long hair
Ain't right. None of my boys ever had that."
I swallowed my response--had none.
One day when I was nineteen
I visited him in his hospital room,
Watched as the nurses
Hooked him up to some god-awful
Machine that forced air into his lungs.
He said nothing
That day, couldn't say anything, but I could.
The last thing he ever heard
Me say: "I love you, Papa."
He died the next day.
Jesus, I need to quit smoking.

ANNE HARDING WOODWORTH is the author of three books of poetry and has recently completed a novella in verse about the friendship of two NASCAR fans. Her poetry has been published in many journals, including *Painted Bride Quarterly*, *Cimarron Review*, *Potomac Review* and *Tiferet*, as well as at several sites on line. Her essays have appeared in *The New York Times*, *The Washington Post* and in various anthologies. She has an M.F.A. in poetry from Fairleigh Dickinson University and is a member of the Folger Shakespeare Library's Poetry Board in Washington, D.C.

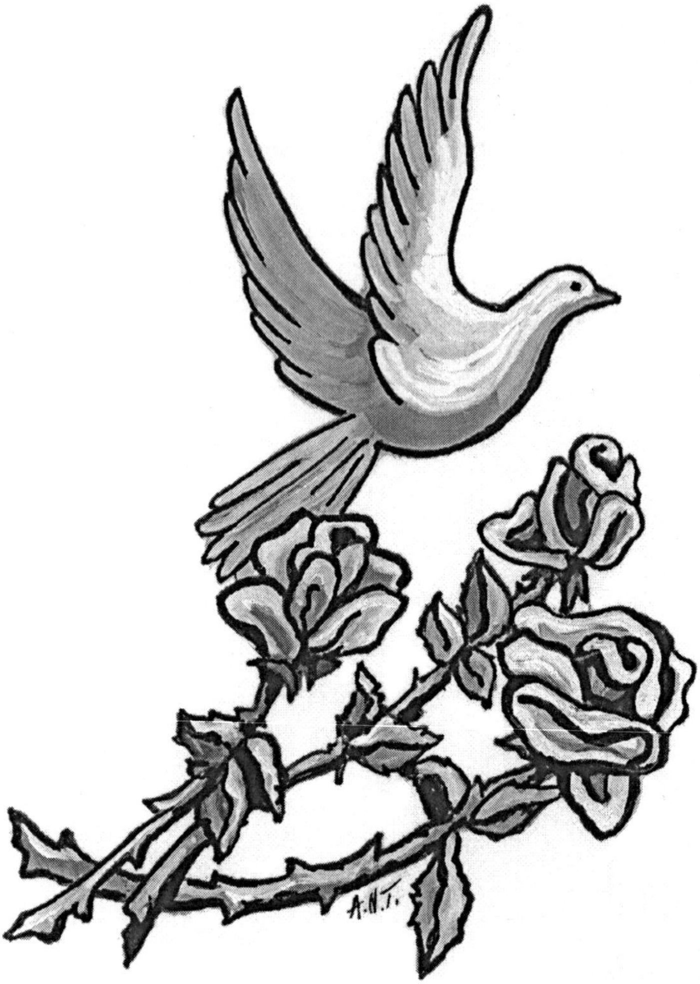
A.N.T.

THE AUDIT

Sinclair Mortimer called a meeting of the Commission to make the final decisions based on the recent audits, as they referred to them.

He scheduled it for Tuesday, August 16, the day after Assumption, when Marys would have celebrated and been blessed, and although Commissioner Mortimer knew he should not mix religion with his job, he thought it was a nice touch for the families involved.

There were several Marys assigned to him. Mary Wheeler, for instance, 92.

Mary Wheeler had been at Myrtle Park for seven years. Five and a half of them plus three days had been at government expense. The first year, she paid her own way till all her assets dried up. It was no secret in town that Tanya had hoped for her mother's passing during that year, so that there would be some inheritance left. Alas, the old woman lived on, and the money was gone after eight months.

Tanya filled out the government forms at Commission Headquarters that would allow Mary to continue living at Myrtle Park. Just when federal assistance was about to kick in, the Commission learned of a safe deposit box in Mary's name in an obscure bank in the South. Of course, it had to be drilled open and its contents analyzed before the federal funds could begin covering the woman's nursing home expenses. In the box a Patek Philippe watch had ceased its ticking but nonetheless gave Mary six more months out of her own purse.

At that point, the rather pretty, silver-haired, soft-skinned woman had not yet tried to get in bed with any of the male residents. Though too frail to keep house alone, she was a sweet and enjoyable person, whom the associates and residents alike treated with kindness. She was what the associates called an easy one. Her room was filled with photos of Tanya and Jim and of their son Roy and his children. Newspaper clippings were pinned on a bulletin board next to her bed. She followed what was going on in government circles, and having been a teacher many years back, she read education columns and the funnies. A small rubber doll in a red dress sat patiently on the shelf behind her bed. Mary hardly noticed it and had long forgotten that the ladies of Holy Name Church had brought it to her one Sunday afternoon.

Mary was cheerily mobile and walked, almost ran, though her footing was always unsure, around the halls of Myrtle Park, talking to everyone she passed, popping into other residents' rooms, and saying coherent and chirpy things like, "Hey, there, inmate, how's it going?" which showed the staff that she had a lucid understanding of the situation. She also sang in the halls, and at Christmas she serenaded with a different carol at each resident's door. Only Mr. Caldwell, 84, would shoo her away, but she took the hint, readily demonstrating that she could still discern different behaviors and predilections of others. Mr. Caldwell's deafness precluded his being an audience anyway.

Mary was deaf, too, but she didn't let it stop her (she wore a hearing aid), and she often said she liked the way she sounded inside her head when she sang.

Sinclair Mortimer, like the other four regional Commissioners, spent his time making rounds to the various geriatric facilities in the area. Once he opened a file on a resident, he recorded (with a redundancy he was known for) exactly what the "aged old-timer" did at every turn, and he watched that person with the "hawk eye of a caracara," as he put it to his golf buddies. His files grew daily, sometimes by the hour, in his efforts to fulfill his duty to the government and his fellow taxpayers. He did it with the detail of monastic illumination, recording the slightest report of variation in a person's urine, stool, epidermis or vocabulary.

He noted for instance that Mary Wheeler "experienced enuresis" for the first time on a certain November 19, and besides that, "she was incontinent." He okayed the extra expense to the government for special underwear. Sinclair also knew exactly, to the minute, when Mary recalled incorrectly her husband's name.

Mary and Tom Wheeler used to sing in the Holy Name choir, as her father Ezra had before them. On their way to practice one Thursday evening, Tom slammed the car into a parking meter just shy of the intersection where a light had turned green. His license had expired years earlier, so it was just as well he died in the accident. What made him swerve like that was anybody's guess, but Mary believed it was the car's shimmy; and whenever she told the story, she would shake her whole body like a shimmying steering shaft. Mary was knocked unconscious in the accident and never sang again till she got to Myrtle Park.

When she was complimented on her singing during the first few years at the home, she acknowledged the praise with grace, saying that everything she'd learned in the voice department she'd learned from Tom. Then one day when Sinclair was making his rounds—it was was a December 17, 12:31 P.M., right after lunch—she said she'd learned her voice technique from Ezra. The next day, Sinclair watched from a distance as Mary shimmied in the re-telling of Tom's death. Sinclair noted in Mary's file that late onset Parkinson's was aggravating the subject's "memory loss and forgetfulness." He scrawled these things down as fast as he could on his clipboard and made a note to watch the old woman carefully from there on. This development placed her in his files as a "Code Pink," which meant the associates were now responsible to report the slightest deviation from the patient's norm. (Residents called them "spy-associates.") Scrupulous documentation was essential at this stage of the game. Sinclair always felt grateful for the extra ears and eyes that might speed up the code spectrum from Pink to the inevitable Blue, and he knew it was his ultimate duty to see that it happened in the quickest and most efficient manner possible.

Mary had a phone in her room and was quite adept at using it, even though she had to pump in a 9 before the regular number. Tanya was an area code away, which had changed from the time-honored 313 Mary had carried easily in her head since the '60s—first to a bad enough 810 or 801 and then a few short months later to an unpleasant 568 or 248 or 828, or something like that. Whatever it was, she just tried it, hit or miss, and was soon calling all over the land to people who shared Tanya's number, but not her area code. Mary enjoyed the conversations she had with whoever answered the phone, especially the woman in the far west, who offered to visit her at Myrtle Park when she and her husband drove cross-country in their RV, which Mary called a TV in relating the story to one of the spy-associates. Tanya, who with little relish paid Mary's phone bill every month, went ballistic when she saw the latest bill and in the heat of the moment ripped the phone out of the wall, fulminating against her mother to a fare-thee-well. She told Sinclair about it, half-thinking he'd offer federal funds for the obviously erroneous bill, but instead he told her she mustn't worry about a little incident like that and gleefully recounted it in Mary's file ("misdials incorrectly and fails to remember area codes") as yet another example on the road to Blue. Tanya paid the $174 bill and didn't buy any Russell Stover assorted creams for her mother for the next several months.

Mary could handle only the creams because she had lost her upper bridge. Sinclair sensed incipient paranoia when a spy-associate told him Mary suspected theft of her upper. Shortly after that, another associate told him Mary had flushed her hearing aid down the toilet and was threatening to stop singing if the person who took it didn't return it. The flushing incident was also recorded but not reversed when Mr. Caldwell "disappeared," as the residents called it, and Mary's hearing aid was found in his left ear under his long white hair. True, he hadn't shooed her away when she stopped by to sing to him during his last days. She had also crawled into his bed for a final warming up. (When Sinclair was informed, he noted in Mary's and Mr. Caldwell's files a diagnosis of "promiscuity and lust," which could be a major factor in the code progression.)

The upper bridge remained at large.

Eating became uninteresting to Mary. She drank some milk, but in spite of it she was shortening up rapidly. This caused walking troubles. A cane was useless, and a walker required too much upper body, which was also shriveling. So she gave in to a wheelchair full time, kicking the footrests up and using her tiptoes in tiny white Keds as her means of propulsion through the halls of Myrtle Park.

On a May 20, at 9:37 a.m., Mary, having been bathed, dressed, combed, put in her wheelchair, did not leave her room. Instead, she said not a word, ingested not a morsel until an associate propped her mouth open with a spoon loaded with applesauce that concealed a diuretic pill. The associate then reported Mary's strange turn of behavior to Sinclair. This was the first day Mary sat looking at air. When an associate offered the rubber doll from the shelf to her, she held it like a young mother in the crook of her elbow, but her eyes were dark and filmy, receding into their sockets. When Tanya visited, infrequent as her visits were becoming, Mary did not stir. She maintained silence for nine straight weeks.

At the beginning of the tenth, almost imperceptibly, a crackly staccato sound exhaled from her toothless once-singing mouth. With time, the noise became a lowing, losing its staccato-like droplets that finally form a steady stream out of an oilcan. The noise grew louder and more constant, even when another human being was nearby. Sinclair sighed with a smug smile: full-blown code Blue.

Assumption came and left like an airy hint of cooked broccoli, unnoticed by the infirm, sniffed by the sound of mind, and celebrated by the hungry.

"As you know," Sinclair began at Headquarters, when the Commissioners had convened on that August 16, "we have several ripe and ready ones this week. The finished audits are complete, and I'd like to get your signatures today, if I might. Now let me go over each individual case, so you know what we're dealing with here. There's Marietta Cornog, Maria Barrueta, Mary Wheeler."

"Whoa, hold the phone, Brother Sinclair," Commissioner Pappas said, chewing gum to stave off his smoking urge in a smoke-free environment. "Ya' think we don't trust ya', fella? We know you know your people. We know you know your guidelines. Jiminy, we all know what our quotas are these days, and it looks like you're makin' some real headway there. You're lookin' for a medal, aren't ya', guy? Come on, now, let's get the things signed and adjourn this meetin'." He stood up and swung an imaginary golf club. All five Commissioners silently watched the perfect ball sail out the window into the firmament beyond.

Sinclair brought the meeting back to order by clearing his throat. "You know, guys, it's interesting," he said. "Three Marys are being signed off on today, the day after Assumption. A trinity of Marys, you might say." He knew his colleagues were all ushers at Holy Name, and he felt sure—though there seemed to be some tension in the room—that they wouldn't report him for bringing religion into a meeting at a federal office. None of them responded to his observation, however. Instead, each one took a pen out of a breast pocket.

The next day Sinclair called Tanya and told her he had the signatures. "And now, young lady, I need your John Hancock signature for the end finalization process to be completed." In spite of the telephone bill incident and having to buy clothes for her mother like cotton athletic suits, Tanya was reluctant to agree. Sinclair had met this problem before.

"Of course, Tanya, once we sign off on her but the family refuses, the cost of her upkeep reverts to the next of kin, who I believe is you. Your mother's had five and a half years on us and we've dutifully paid her bills to Myrtle Park, which has been a fine place for her until now as far as the government's concerned."

Tanya was crying and saying something about carrying all that guilt on her shoulders for the rest of her life. Sinclair, having heard that one, too, and being adept at shifting burdens, said, "You? Guilty? Folderol, young lady. You're being a kind and loving daughter. You're doing for her what you'd want Roy to do for you." He had met Tanya's son and had just recently seen him across the aisle on a flight to the nation's capital. The young father of two had a blond tail down the back of his neck, and he was wearing shorts, a tank top, earphones, and flip-flops. Sinclair knew the mention of her vacuous son would give Tanya a fresh view of her own acuity. She would never let herself be in a situation where Roy would be called upon to sign his name to such a document. Women like Tanya, Sinclair knew, always decide it'll be completely different when their time comes. They don't see themselves in places like Myrtle Park or in situations in any way like Mary's. So, bearing the burden of her present responsibility rather stalwartly and wanting to get on with her own life that would keep her far from a finish in a Myrtle Park at the hands of an obtuse son, Tanya signed.

"With assurance and confidence," Sinclair noted in the file.

The next morning an associate entered Mary's room earlier than usual. She dressed the little woman in someone else's frayed, oil-stained athletic suit and Keds. She did not comb Mary's hair. A cart arrived outside the door, and a man went directly to Mary's closet to remove every piece of clothing, four old purses, a jacket, a pitch pipe. In the far back he found an upper bridge of five teeth and laughed as he held it up for the associate to see. He pitched it across the room into the trash bin. He took down all the pictures on the shelf behind Mary's bed and the cards and photos and clippings on the bulletin board. He put all that on the cart. The daughter would be around later in the week to collect everything but the athletic suits, he'd heard, which would be provided to other Pinks and Blues.

Mary, sitting in her wheelchair, was staring into air. When the teeth arced over her head on their way to the bin, her tongue—as if remembering something—appeared to slink out around her gray lips and in turn she exhaled her first lowing of the day. It took on a hollow, mournful sound, a wail that echoed out of her room and down the hall. She was otherwise docile, in no way curious about the emptying of her holding receptacles, and when the associate inoculated her with a sedative, her chin dropped down onto her brittle left collarbone.

"Okay, Mary, darlin', this is it. Say goodbye to your friends here at Myrtle Park," the associate said, and she pushed Mary out of the room she had lived in for seven years, down the hall to the elevator, down to the "box" as the staff called it, usually in jest, sometimes as a playful threat to each other.

There Mary "passed away for this great country of ours, a fine patriot, one who contributed loyally to the welfare of her family and her fellow-citizens in ways too numerous to enumerate," Sinclair wrote later that morning in Mary's file.

Tanya dropped by the next day to collect the urn and the articles of her mother's life on earth.

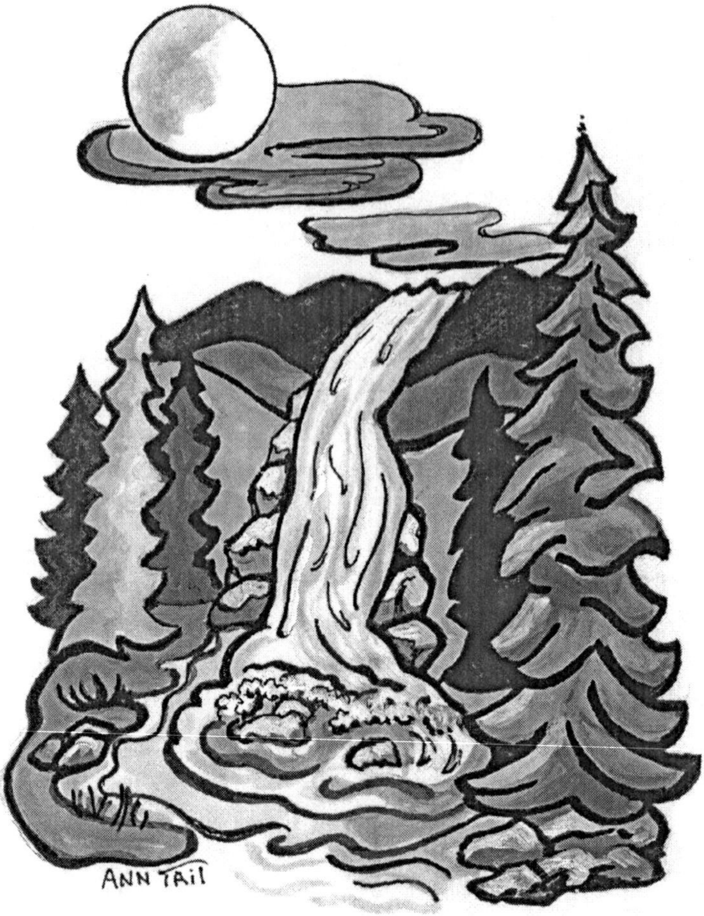
ANN TAIT

Made in the USA